V1

BMR
S/O
8-99

BEGGAR MAID, QUEEN

Anne Neville, daughter of Warwick the Kingmaker, was destined to know the most amazing switches of fortune before she became Queen of England and wife to King Richard III. This novel traces her strange history from the security of her beloved home at Middleham to the war-tents of Margaret of Anjou, from the slums of London to its palaces. Anne's nature and the course of her life are shaped when, from her nursery window, she sees a young boy riding through the postern gate . . .

MAUREEN PETERS

◆

BEGGAR MAID, QUEEN

Complete and Unabridged

LINFORD
Leicester

SAN/00 15888 (1/00

First published in Great Britain in 1980 by
Robert Hale Limited
London

First Linford Edition
published 2000
by arrangement with
Robert Hale Limited
London

British Library CIP Data

Peters, Maureen, *1935* –
    Beggar maid, queen.—Large print ed.—
Linford romance library
1. Love stories
2. Large type books
I. Title
823.9'14 [F]

ISBN 0–7089–5779–X

Published by
F. A. Thorpe (Publishing)
Anstey, Leicestershire

Set by Words & Graphics Ltd.
Anstey, Leicestershire
Printed and bound in Great Britain by
T. J. International Ltd., Padstow, Cornwall

This book is printed on acid-free paper

1

From the window seat she could look down over the drawbridge towards the road that wound steeply to the village below. There were always people coming and going between Middleham and York, and from her high vantage-point they looked like dolls. The knights in their steel helmets and breastplates were tiny enough to be picked up in one hand and their horses were even smaller than the ones in her toy farm.

'If I were a giant child,' Anne said aloud, 'I could put my arm out of the window and pick up all those people.'

'Lord, what strange notions you do have!' Ankarette exclaimed.

'My father said I was a changeling child,' Anne remarked, nose still pressed against the window pane. 'What is a changeling child, Nurse?'

'One left by the fairies when they

steal a human babe,' Ankarette said, placidly knitting.

'Oh.' Anne considered the question for a moment, then said gravely, 'I had liefer be the Earl of Warwick's daughter.'

'As you are, my pet.' Ankarette raised her head and smiled across the room at her charge. ''Tis only that you're small for your age, but you'll grow soon enough.'

'I hope so.' Anne sighed a little, for at five years old she was generally mistaken for three, and in a tall, elegant family she was noticeably tiny. When she was in company all that she could see, unless she tilted back her head, were legs and long, trailing skirts. For that reason she liked to sit up high, where she could look down and see faces as well. Faces intrigued her, because so often the expressions on them didn't match the thoughts she could sense churned behind the polite outward smile.

Her own face was small and pointed,

the dark eyes slightly tilted at the corners and her brown hair hung in two thick braids from beneath the white lace coif. It was no wonder that her father had called her a changeling, she thought. The Earl of Warwick and his Countess were big and blond, and her sister Isobel was, at nine, always wearing a dress in the latest fashion, with a train to be looped over the arm.

Anne glanced down at her own dress with a curling lip. Its scalloped hem ended only four inches below her knees and its red silk was unadorned save for narrow bands of black velvet at wrists and neck. She would have liked a tall hennin with a veil floating out behind, and wooden pattens under the soles of her red leather shoes.

The procession winding its way up the hill was nearing the drawbridge. Men-at-arms, pikes in their hands, rode closely about a small, cloaked figure.

'Ankarette, there is a boy coming,' she said. 'He looks like an important boy.'

Ankarette put aside her knitting and came over to the window.

'Why, I should think he is,' she said. 'That must be the Duke of Gloucester, King Edward's youngest brother. I heard that he was being sent here to complete his education.'

'I have never seen him before,' Anne, who since babyhood had spent a good portion of her life jogging between her father's Yorkshire household and his larger castle at Warwick, craned her neck to see. 'Is he a kinsman?'

'King Edward is your father's cousin, which makes his brother a cousin too,' Ankarette said. 'Their mother, Dame Cecily, is a Neville and you are a Neville too.'

Anne nodded, wrinkling her smooth brow. There were so many relatives coming and going, all of them talking in loud, confident voices, few of them taking any notice of her at all, for all that she was the daughter of the most powerful nobleman in the land. Sometimes she became extremely confused

4

as to who was who and which people were friendly to her family. The Percies, for example, supported King Henry and Queen Margaret whom her father had driven from the throne, but young Robert Percy was being educated at Middleham and nobody seemed to mind that his family had chosen the wrong side.

'You will have to go down,' Ankarette said.

'Must I?' Anne twisted around and looked pleadingly at her nurse. 'Nobody will miss me.'

'Of course you must go down! Where are your manners?'

Ankarette lifted her to the floor and smoothed down her dress, her glance anxiously loving. Anne was the favourite of her two charges, though she would not have admitted it. She took another look through the window, but the riders were clattering across the drawbridge into the covered way.

'Go down now and greet the Duke,' she said again.

Anne trotted obediently out of the room and down the twisting stairs. As always the delicious scent of fresh bread rose to her nostrils. At Middleham the nursery was over the bakehouse on the north side of the courtyard, and the cook generally saved a bit of ginger-bread, or a finger of cinnamon cake for Anne. Today she virtuously shook her head, and went out into the courtyard, in time to see the tail-end of the procession on its way through to the eastern courtyard, where the stables were.

The boy had dismounted and stood, bareheaded, drinking from the welcome cup that the Countess had offered. For a moment Anne hesitated, watching the tableau outside the open doors of the Great Hall. Her mother was in a fashionable high-waisted gown of green velvet, its hanging sleeves lined with silver. Her head was tilted back slightly by the weight of her enormous butterfly headdress, and diamonds sparkled at her throat and ears. Her brows had been plucked to a thin line and her eyelids were painted with green malacite.

At her side the Earl stood in a characteristic stance, legs apart, thumbs hooked into the jewelled belt of his scarlet gown. Furred sleeves hung in points to the cobblestones and a feathered cap was clamped to the side of his head. At 32 the Earl of Warwick was at the zenith of his influence and wealth, and it was reflected in his bearing.

Nine-year-old Isobel was by her mother, fair curls bouncing on her shoulders, her face powdered white. Already she was a replica of the Countess, her train looped over her arm, a wreath of tiny silver flowers on her head. She was already a beauty, Anne thought with a little twinge of wistful envy.

The boy was shorter than those who greeted him, his black hair hanging limply to the collar of his turquoise doublet, his legs thin stalks of scarlet silk. A cloak of white velvet was being put about his narrow shoulders to replace the black travelling cape, and a jewelled scabbard hung from his belt. In contrast to the splendour of his garments his profile was grave and sallow.

The Countess, seeing Anne, beckoned impatiently, and Anne went swiftly to her side, dipping into a curtsy as she had been trained.

'Richard, this is the younger of my two daughters,' the Earl said, putting out a hand and drawing the little girl closer to him.

'God give you greeting, Lady Anne,' the boy bowed.

Impressed by the fact that he had remembered her name without any prompting Anne gazed at him. He was not a handsome boy. His face was narrow and had not yet filled out sufficiently to accommodate his long nose, but he had dark eyes that tilted up at the corners like her own and his voice was pleasant.

They were going into the Great Hall, and Anne was swept along with the rest of them. Here other members of the household waited to be introduced, and a knot of younglings, with whom the newcomer would share lodgings and instruction, were eyeing the Duke with interest.

The Great Hall was an immense apartment, warmed at each end by enormous fires, its 12-foot thick walls hung with tapestries. Although it was mild for November the afternoon light was already fading and hundreds of waxen tapers had been lit in the iron sconces that hung by chains from the rafters. The remaining light slanted through the double doors and the high, narrow windows, illuminating the few pieces of dark, heavily carved furniture, the massive cupboard whose shelves were crammed with gold and silver plate, the long trestle tables with their white cloths and varied array of sweet and savoury dishes. Halfway up one wall was the minstrel's gallery, reached by a narrow staircase, and Anne mounted this and settled herself comfortably where she could look down on everybody.

She was not yet of an age to eat in the hall, taking her meals with Ankarette in the nursery, but she liked to watch the other people as they took their places or moved up and down with trays and jugs.

The Duke had been seated between her parents as a mark of favour and because it was his first evening. After today he would join the other boys. They had their own dormitory over the schoolroom and were to be heard every morning loudly declaiming their Latin verbs. They took turns to serve at table at the dinner-hour, and afterwards, in their small suits of armour, they rode out into the surrounding moors to practise the more vigorous arts of sword and axe fighting, shooting at the butts and hawking.

They were also expected to make polite conversation and dance with the

Earl's daughters and any other young lady who chanced to be visiting. Isobel had already been the recipient of several ink-stained poems and favours tied with bits of ribbon, but the boys never noticed Anne except to tug her long braids in passing.

The Duke looked tired and pale after his journey. Anne noticed that he ate sparingly and scarcely touched his goblet of wine. She noticed too that he held his left shoulder a trifle hunched as if it were a habit. Once or twice he smiled in response to some remark of the Earl's, and then his sallow face lit up charmingly.

It was impossible to hear any of the conversation. There was a general babble in the hall and a clattering of dishes as each course was borne in and then removed. Below the salt the menials craned their necks to look at the new arrival and then, finding nothing of interest, returned to their own gossip. The Earl, despite the great state he kept, prided himself on the freedom of speech he allowed his retainers, secure in the knowledge that his liberality had made him popular. Any friend of one of the Earl's servants was entitled to enter the kitchens and carry away as much meat as he could spear on the point of his dagger.

The meal was drawing to its close with bowls of comfits and sugared almonds being handed round while the company broke up into smaller groups, some moving near the great fires where stools had been placed for the ladies, others standing with their goblets in tight circles of gossip. No doubt many would be passing comment on the Duke, and the Duke himself was evidently aware of the fact, for Anne saw him glance around in a slightly self-conscious manner. Then he took a handful of sugared almonds from a proffered bowl and began to walk towards the staircase on which Anne was perched.

She shrank a little, waiting for the

teasing word, the comment on her size, but the boy sat down on the step below her and, turning, took one of her hands and emptied the pink and white dainties into her palm.

'My father does not allow me to eat many sweetmeats,' she said nervously. 'He says they rot the teeth.'

'Only the second teeth,' the boy said gravely. 'Anyway, your father is an earl and I am a duke, so my wish takes precedence.'

Anne knew about precedence. It had to do with making certain that people were in their correct places. Sometimes there were arguments and two ladies would collide in a doorway, the horns of their hennins locked together like stags in combat.

'I will save them if it please you,' she said shyly.

'As you please, Lady Anne.' He gave her his sudden, heart-lifting smile and she reddened with pleasure. To hide it she bent her head and began to count the almonds,

13

'Rich man, poor man, beggar man, thief.'

'No, lady.' His hand, long-fingered and sunburned, reached out and held her wrist. 'Rich maid, poor maid, beggar maid, queen. That is how your rhyme shall go.'

'Did you make it up out of your head?' she asked, impressed.

'In our family we make up everything to suit ourselves,' he said wryly.

'You come from a large family,' she ventured, trying to remember what she had been told of them.

'There is my sister, Anne, who is Duchess of Exeter.' He counted them off on his fingers. 'Then there is His Grace King Edward.'

'Whom God defend,' Anne said piously, as she had been taught.

'Amen to that! And then there is Elizabeth. She wed the Duke of Suffolk a year ago. Then there is Margaret. Then George, who is 12 years old, and then myself.'

'Six of you.'

'There were others,' he said, a shadow coming over his face. 'My brother Edmund was killed last year at Wakefield by that fiend, Margaret of Anjou. He and my father, both killed and their heads spiked over York's gateway.'

'I was in Warwick then,' Anne said apologetically.

'And I was in Calais, chained to my books.' He scowled at some private hurt and then said, 'There were those who died as babes too. Henry, William, John, Thomas, Ursula — they all died as babes.'

She saw them in her mind as a row of little, sheeted figures, each with its corpse candle.

'I have only the one sister, Isobel,' she said. 'She is nine years old.'

'As I am.' He smiled at her again and said, 'Eat your almonds. I am going to talk to the other boys now, but I will see you again.'

'Are you staying for a long time?' she asked.

'Until I am of an age to fight and defend my brother's throne,' he said, his child's mouth hardening.

She was silent, nibbling the almonds daintily, her eyes following his small, hunched figure as he moved down into the main body of the hall again.

He was, she thought, stifling a yawn, the nicest boy she had ever met.

The Countess, glancing up and spying her younger daughter, exclaimed at the lateness of the hour, her well-bred voice edged with temper.

'The child will have rings like saucers beneath her eyes! She will be stunted in her growth if she loses her sleep!'

'I'll see to her.' The Earl, mellowed by wine and the arrival of one of the most important children in the kingdom, strode across and lifted his daughter in his arms.

'To bed, to bed, sleepyhead!' His tone was indulgent. 'Where is your nurse?'

'Probably looking for me,' Anne said, snuggling up against her father's broad chest. It was not often that she had the luxury of a few minutes alone with her splendid parent. It was seldom that he was at home with them for more than a few weeks, because he was usually very busy fighting battles that would keep Edward safely on the throne. The trouble was that King Henry and his son were still at large, and there was always the possibility that his fierce French wife would try to wrench back the crown.

'You must be a good girl,' the Earl said absently now, carrying her across the courtyard to the nursery quarters. 'You must do as your nurse tells you. What have you in your hand?'

'Nothing now,' Anne said, hastily stuffing the last almond into her mouth and displaying a sticky palm.

'It will ruin your teeth,' her father said, setting her on her feet. 'Go up to your chamber, maid.'

'Beggar maid, queen,' Anne said.

'What's that?' The Earl looked down at her.

'A rhyme the Duke of Gloucester told to me.'

'Well, you are not likely ever to be either of those things,' he said, bending to tug her braids gently. 'Do you like the Duke?'

'Yes. Oh, yes!' Her voice lilted. 'I like him very much!'

'He is to live with us here for a while. I hope you will make him welcome if he seeks your company.'

The instincts of a court-bred child stirred in her, and she asked tremulously, 'Is there to be a wedding?'

If he mentioned Isobel's name she thought that she would die, but he merely smiled down at her in the gloom and said, 'You're too young to be setting your cap at the gentleman. Grow into a beautiful lady and then we shall see.'

'God give you goodnight,' she said quaintly and trotted within.

Her father gazed after her, stroking his chin thoughtfully. There were occasions when he bitterly deplored the fact that he had only sired two daughters and no male heir, but girls were invaluable counters in the marriage stakes. It was too soon to make definite plans, of course. King Edward could be surprisingly stubborn when it came to the point, but he was only 19 and indebted to his powerful cousin for his throne. That sense of obligation must be lovingly nurtured and, meanwhile, it would be pleasant to have the young Duke about the place. The boy had had an unsettled childhood, being moved from one stronghold to another and twice being exiled to the safety of Calais while the struggle for the throne swayed first one way and then the other way. The Earl would not have taken the crown if it had been offered to him. It was infinitely preferable to be the man who decided who was to wear the bauble.

Ankarette was dozing over her knitting, the flickering light from the candles and the fire casting a rosy glow over her bent head, its red curls covered by a cap of white linen. She was still in her twenties and had a sweetheart whom she intended to wed when she had put aside sufficient for a dowry. Anne hoped that would not be for many years. She could not imagine life without Ankarette.

The two low-ceilinged chambers that comprised the nursery were the little girl's domain. Isobel spent much of her time with the Countess, but Anne liked to steal away to this familiar refuge. Here was the big curtained bed she shared with Isobel, the deep chest where her gowns were laid, the table on which her toy farm was lovingly arranged. Some of the guards had carved the wooden figures and painted them in bright colours. Anne thought dreamily that she would like to have a real farm one day.

The outer door creaked open and Isobel came in, swishing the train of her gown over the rushes and causing Ankarette to jerk awake.

'Lord! I must have been wool-gathering! What time is it?'

'Time for good little girls to be in bed,' Isobel mimicked.

'Aye, so it is, Mistress Clever Tongue.' Ankarette, who was not in the least impressed by the fact that her charges were the richest heiresses in the land, rose, shaking out her full skirts. 'Hurry now, or you'll not be up in time for Mass tomorrow, and that would set a bad example to the little Duke.'

'He is a very dull boy,' Isobel complained, standing still as her wreath of silver flowers was removed. 'I found him a very dull boy.'

'Dukes,' said Ankarette firmly, 'are never dull.'

'He is dark and small and all the rest of his family are big and fair,' Isobel said. 'I saw King Edward once and he was very handsome even though he wasn't a king then, of course.'

'Perhaps he is a changeling,' Anne said brightly.

'Indeed he's no such thing!' Ankarette said, unhooking the child's
bodice. 'And don't go saying such
nonsense in any public place. Richard
of Gloucester is true-born Plantagenet.'

'But the youngest son,' Isobel pointed
out.

'It makes no difference. The King is
said to be devoted to his brothers and
sisters,' Ankarette said.

'And to his cousins,' Isobel said. 'It
was my lord father who helped him to
his throne.'

Anne, wriggling out of her gown,
thought fleetingly of King Edward's
other cousin, the deposed king Henry.
He and his queen had fled first to
Scotland and were now ensconced at
Bamburgh. It was said that Henry had
long since lost his wits and was unfit to
govern anything but Queen Margaret
had plenty of energy and was trying to
make a treaty with the French. Perhaps
it made little difference who sat upon
the throne because the Earl held all the
reins of power anyway. Anne had heard

her father referred to as the Kingmaker, and now she thought, with a little stab of uneasiness, that he was a King-breaker too.

In the months that followed she saw the Duke frequently but found no opportunity to speak to him. He knelt with the other boys at Mass and as Anne was not yet of an age to sup in hall she had no chance of mingling with those who gossiped and danced until the servants came to light them to bed. She did see him often in the tiltyard or at the butts, but he was too intent on his practice to notice her at all. The lads around him laughed and joked when they missed the target or were tumbled backward by the sheer weight of their armour, but the little Duke practised with grim determination, biting his lip when he made an error, always struggling unaided to his feet.

'For all the world as if it were a real conflict and not a mock one,' the Countess said indulgently.

She was in an excellent humour,

having received word that Queen Margaret's small army had been scattered and that three of the biggest Northumbrian castles were under siege. Her husband was personally conducting the campaign, King Edward having succumbed to a most unkingly attack of measles. Nobody was sure where King Henry was, but as he was a cipher anyway it made little difference. Meanwhile she remained quietly at Middleham, guarding her daughters and keeping a maternal eye on young Richard of Gloucester. Once Edward was truly secure on his throne she would contrive a betrothal between the Duke and Anne. It was a pity that the girls were not older else she might have aimed for the King himself, but a foreign alliance was needed there, and the Earl favoured France.

Now she said sharply to Anne, who was trotting along at her side,

'Do take longer steps. Ladies should glide, not bounce up and down!'

'My legs are too short,' Anne panted,

trying to keep pace.

'Nonsense!' The Countess stopped walking and scowled at her daughter.

The girl was certainly tiny and far too thin, she mused. The physician had assured her that Anne was healthy, and Ankarette declared she was very bright at her lessons, but life was uncertain at the best of times and plague or accident could put an end to the most ambitious schemes. For that reason she considered it wiser to rear her daughters amid the healthy, bracing atmosphere of the moors and, on their yearly visits to Warwick Castle, to confine them to the private gardens.

The Duke had seen her and was taking off his helmet and giving her a courteous bow. She smiled at him, thinking with an unaccustomed wistfulness that she would have liked a son, and spoke to him kindly,

'You put great effort into your practice, Richard, but you must take care not to tire yourself out.'

'My brother needs strong fighting

men, madam,' the boy said.

'Ah, you are loyal and that is best of all,' she approved.

'I have taken it for my motto,' the boy said earnestly. 'Loyalty binds me'. Do you think it a good motto?'

'An excellent one.' She smiled at him more warmly than ever.

'I wondered, madam, if there was any news of the campaign.'

'No more than I told you yesterday. You must bear your impatience a while, my dear. The campaign will end in a victory for the Earl,' she said.

'A victory for my brother, surely?' Richard said, his dark eyes suddenly cold.

'Naturally.' The Countess wished her words had not been seized upon so quickly. 'Our fortunes are so bound together that what affects one affects the other.'

'Of course, madam.' The Duke hesitated and then said, 'Is it true I am to visit the King next year?'

'You are invited to the Court,' she

nodded. 'You will wish to see your mother again, and your other brothers and sisters.'

'Could the Lady Anne come too?' he asked.

The Countess cast an astonished glance at her daughter. Anne's peaky little face had flushed scarlet and her eyes were like stars. She looked almost pretty, her mother reflected. Who would have thought that she had caught the little Duke's attention! The feelings of the two children were not, of course, of the smallest importance when their possible betrothal was discussed, but it was always more convenient when bride and bridegroom were in accord. The Countess, who had been wed to the Earl at the age of nine, had never been in love in her life, but she regarded her marriage as an eminently successful one. The Earl's aunt was King Edward's mother, and in the Countess's own veins ran the blood of old John of Gaunt. Their joint lands were larger and more prosperous than any others in

England, and their ambitions marched together. She could not recall their ever having exchanged a cross word.

'Anne is far too young to be taken to Court,' she said, 'especially when the times are so difficult. You will only be away for a few months, Richard, and when you return you will be bringing the Duke of Clarence for a visit to us.'

George at 13 would be a useful lad to cultivate, especially if he could be induced to look at Isobel in the same way that Richard was now looking at Anne. The Countess smiled at them both even more kindly than before.

'I would like to go to Court,' Anne piped up.

'When you are older, dear,' her mother said, in a tone almost as indulgent as the Earl's might have been.

Anne gave Richard a pleading glance, but he being too well-bred to argue bowed politely and returned to his companions, putting on his helmet again as he went.

Going away for months. The phrase

echoed dismally in Anne's mind and her feet dragged as she trailed after her mother. Months stretched out for ever and it was hard to remember people for such a long time. It was likely, she thought dismally, that Richard of Gloucester would forget her altogether while he was at Court.

2

It had been a wonderful season. Anne went over and over it in her mind, remembering the gaieties of the 12 days of feasting that succeeded the festival of the Nativity. The Duke of Gloucester had not forgotten her. That was the one shining fact that stood out among all the rest. He had not forgotten her and she had not forgotten him. When the royal party had ridden into the courtyard of Middleham her eyes had flown at once to the slight figure in the black velvet cloak, the green tunic so thickly sewn with gold that it was hard to see the material beneath.

'Make your curtsy to His Grace,' her mother had hissed, poking her in the back, and she had hastily knelt, the cobblestones sharp through the thin satin of her dress, and heard a pleasant, deep voice exclaim,

'So this is Lady Anne! I saw you when you were a babe but you'll not remember it.'

King Edward was bending from his great height to raise her to her feet. He was the tallest man she had ever seen, with fair hair waving to his shoulders and bright blue eyes. He was even bigger than her father, she thought in awe, and the great King laughed down at her as if he understood exactly how she felt, and said,

'Why, she is a rose, my lady of Warwick! A veritable rose!'

'She is a good child,' the Earl said fondly.

He was himself in high good humour, the three Northumbrian castles having surrendered, and Queen Margaret having taken her son and fled to her father's court in Anjou. Nobody was sure where poor, witless King Henry was, and nobody was particularly concerned.

'How old is she?' the King was asking.

'She will be eight next year,' the Countess said.

'We must have her at Court some time,' Edward said, turning to bring forward a tall, fair boy so remarkably like himself in appearance that it could only be the Duke of Clarence. George of Clarence made his bow to her with marked indifference and soon slipped away to ogle Isobel, who was looking especially pleasing in a high-waisted gown of sapphire blue.

Richard was bowing before her and she heard him inquire formerly after her health, but the words they used were of no importance. She could tell from his eyes and the pucker of laughter at the side of his mouth that he had not forgotten her and that he was very pleased to be back at Middleham.

Everybody ate in the hall at Yuletide, the immediate family occupying seats on the dais, the others taking their places according to rank, with the menials crammed together below the salt. Anne had a thick cushion placed under her so that she could reach the table properly and, whether by accident or design, she was placed within speaking distance of Richard. He leaned over to cut up the piece of meat on her plate and she sat, her hands folded demurely within the wide sleeves of her pink dress, and forgot how earnestly she had begged for a train and a steeple hennin.

'Was London interesting?' she asked shyly.

'Overcrowded and stinking,' he said briefly. 'I like the north better.'

Under the pink bodice her flat little chest swelled. What he was really saying was that he liked the north because she was in it. She lifted her goblet of wine carefully in both hands and offered it to him as she had seen her mother do to an honoured guest, and he took it and drank from it. Farther down the table George of Clarence and Isobel had their heads together and were giggling.

The Earl, slanting a glance towards his wife, who acknowledged it with a barely perceptible lifting of her plucked brows, thought, for perhaps the first time, that he was fortunate not to have a son. Sons in the line of succession had uncomfortable and frequently short lives, but daughters could be married off. His glance shifted to Edward, who was flattering the Countess outrageously. It was time to cement the proposed alliance with France by a marriage with the princess, Bona, who was sister-in-law to King Louis. The alliance would drive a wedge between Scotland and France and ensure that Queen Margaret had no friends whom she could bully into invading England on her witless husband's behalf.

'My brother has done well at his lessons and his knightly training, I believe?' Edward said.

'Exceptionally well, my liege,' the Earl made haste to answer. 'He has been most diligent.'

'I shall leave him with you for a few months longer,' Edward said, 'but good conduct deserves a reward, don't you agree, my lord Warwick?'

'Indeed it does,' the Earl said solemnly.

He knew exactly what was coming, having discussed the entire matter with his royal cousin previously.

'Richard, stand up in your place!' Edward called.

The boy rose at once as the Earl banged on the table for silence.

'Richard, Duke of Gloucester, in token of your hard work and sober conduct, I confer upon you the dignity of High Admiral of Ireland, England and Aquitaine,' Edward announced in ringing tones.

Richard's sallow complexion flushed darkly with pleasure, but George of Clarence's voice rose shrilly above the murmurs of approval.

'That isn't fair! He is only 11 years old and has done nothing!'

'And I appoint you Constable of Corfe Castle,' Edward continued, with a warning glance at George.

'I am most grateful, sire,' Richard said.

'And so you should be!' George exploded. 'Why, you have done absolutely nothing to earn those honours!'

'But I shall do,' Richard said. He was still on his feet, his eyes fixed unswervingly on his brother the King.

'Promises, promises,' George said sulkily.

'I am giving you the lordship of Pembroke,' Edward told him.

'I thank you, my liege.' George had the grace to look faintly ashamed of himself, and Isobel flashed him a look of deep sympathy.

Anne was staring down at her plate. Part of her was pleased for Richard's sake, and part of her was sorry for the older boy who had received a set-down in public. Perhaps he had deserved it, but she was sorry for him all the same. So sorry that a tear trickled down the side of her nose and plopped into the gravy. She wiped it away and, looking up, saw the King's blue eyes fixed on her.

'Did you want a reward too?' he asked.

'Oh, no, thank you!' she exclaimed in dismay. 'I'm too little to be an admiral.'

Laughter rippled through the assembled guests, and she found herself joining in without quite knowing why. The slight unpleasantness was wiped from her mind, and she felt as if Yuletide had begun.

The Earl kept high state in whatever castle he happened to be residing, but at the birthday of the Christ Child formal etiquette was mitigated by a good deal of merrymaking under the Lord of Misrule.

The King had elected himself as Lord of Misrule and he directed the entertainments with so much enthusiasm that it was hard to remember he had a throne to secure and a kingdom to rule. There were jousts, and sledge-rides down the hill with tiny bells jangling on the horses' collars. At Mass they sang carols, and the villagers traipsed up the steep hill to receive bread, meat and wine from the ladies of the household, and in the evening she was allowed to stay up late and join in the dancing and the games of Hoodman blind and Bell the Cat. Anne was not at ease when their was too much horseplay. Some of the squires forgot their training in polite etiquette and became too rough. She liked better the quieter games when they played Spelling Bee and rolled dice for gifts of small trinkets, and she liked best of all the hours when the whole household gathered round the fire while the Earl told ghost stories or the minstrels played softly in the gallery above.

There had been one enchanted hour when she and Richard had stolen away together up into the nursery and, with Ankarette enjoying herself in the arms of her betrothed over in the stables, the two of them had played with her wooden farm. It had not been an entirely satisfactory game because Richard had turned the farm into a fort and had a battle between the animals that ended up with the pigs being victorious.

'Because my emblem is the white boar,' he had explained.

'And mine is the bear holding a ragged staff,' Anne said.

'They don't have bears on a farm,' Richard said with unanswerable logic.

'Oh, but I am very glad the boar won,' she said hastily, and he laughed and set her animals in order, waving his thin brown hand over them as he pronounced them alive again.

There was some gingerbread down in the bakehouse and she went and got some for them both, breaking it into pieces and sharing it between them as they sat together on the window-seat. The light was dying, but in the courtyard the figures of the King and the Earl could be glimpsed pacing up and down, deep in conversation. From up here neither of them looked tall or formidable, and the boy and girl drew closer, munching their gingerbread, enjoying the clandestine thrill of watching their elders without themselves being observed.

'Will you leave in a few months and go south to the Court?' Anne asked.

'When the spring turns into summer,' he said.

That was months and months ahead, she thought happily, and snuggled closer. Being with Richard was a warm, safe feeling, like being with Ankarette but better. She swallowed the last delicious crumb of gingerbread and said,

'I wonder what they are talking about down there.'

'About my brother's marriage to Bona of Savoy,' Richard said, 'and the treaty with France. Big, important matters.'

'If I could have anything in the world,' Anne said impulsively, 'I would ask for a real farm with real animals. I would get up in the morning and milk my own cow, and then go out into the fields with my own sheep.'

'They wouldn't let you have a farm,'

Richard said, 'and you'd not like it if they did. All the milkmaids I ever saw had chilblains on their fingers and thick ankles and smelled of dung. Now your hands are white and your ankles slim and you smell like a — '

'Like a rose?' she asked hopefully, but he shook his head.

'Lots of ladies smell of roses,' he said. 'It's the perfume they use. No, you smell like a flower I once found in a crevice of the moors when we were out hawking. Above the snowline it was, almost invisible in the grass. It was blue, with little streaks of white on the petals, and it smelled faint and sweet. It was like you, Anne. I almost picked it for you, but it wouldn't have lasted away from where it grew, so I let it be.'

'I would like to come to Court when I am a woman grown,' she said, feeling obscurely troubled.

'I shall come to Yorkshire before that time,' he said, gravely as if he were making a solemn vow. 'I shall come back and find you, Anne.'

41

They clasped hands briefly and then the bell clanged the supper-hour and their time of privacy was over. She held it in her memory like a perfect and shining jewel and made no effort to seek his sole company again. Perfection ought to come in small portions so that it couldn't overwhelm one.

The festivities over, the King rode away with the Earl at his side, and George of Clarence bringing up the rear. Anne was rather glad that George was going. He was, she considered privately, a spoilt, greedy lad for all his handsome looks. Isobel and he had spent a lot of time together and excited much admiration with their dancing. Anne, bobbing solemnly up and down with Richard in the corner, had glanced enviously at the tall, fair younglings as they glided about under the approving gaze of their elders.

The season had been shorter than she expected. Within a month of their departure word had come that Prince Richard, Duke of Gloucester, was to join the King at Leicester, taking with him those men willing to fight in Edward's cause.

'For the Duke of Somerset has raised forces for King Henry, and it is necessary for them to be scattered and defeated,' Richard explained.

He had insisted on donning full armour and clanked about with a grave expression on his narrow face. Anne, watching, thought he looked very warlike and splendid, though he would not be 12 until October.

'We shall pray for your safety,' the Countess said with equal gravity. 'You will not forget us here?'

'I will not forget,' he said and bowed as gracefully as possible in his jointed metal suit before clanking to the mountaing block to be hoisted into the saddle.

He had said that he would not forget and she believed him completely. She would always believe what he told her, she promised herself, and when he saw her again she would know that he had never forgotten her.

'You need not fret,' the Countess said, giving her a kindly look as the procession began to form up in preparation for the ride out across the drawbridge and down the steep road to the village. 'Richard is too young to take part in any fighting. No harm will come to him.'

'It is not yet his time,' Anne said, and the Countess shivered, a cold breeze lifting the little hairs at the back of her neck.

'You'd better go indoors,' she said, and Anne went obediently, without glancing at the small, armoured figure again.

In the spring Ankarette was married, clad in a gown of white samite with a lace veil that the Countess had given her. She looked beautiful, Anne thought, and tried not to remember that the bride would be going to her husband's home in Somerset, and that in future she would be in the charge of the Countess. The nursery was for little girls and Anne was eight and must begin her education proper, with regular lessons, and a lute master to teach her how to play the mellow toned instrument, and a dancing master to teach her the latest steps. She and Isobel would sit in the family solar at their embroidery frames, and eat at the high table in hall every day, and there would be no Ankarette to wake her from terror when she rode the night mare on full moon nights. For a moment tears threatened, but she blinked them back resolutely. It would be selfish to spoil Ankarette's day.

The bride went off with her beaming husband and word of a decisive victory against the rebel forces marked the beginning of summer when the surrounding moors were purpled with heather and the brown streams gilded by the sun. She liked to ride her pony on the slopes below the high crags, but she never caught sight of the blue flower the little Duke had described. It was a peaceful season, and the only thing she regretted was that she grew so slowly. Isobel was head and shoulders above her and had a definite bust whereas Anne was not only tiny but as thin as ever. She consoled herself with the reflection that it would be dreadful if she grew even taller than Richard. She was sure that one of his main reasons for liking her was because, in a tall and powerfully built family, she, like him, was small and insignificant.

'The summer will be over soon,' the Countess said one day as they sat at their needlework. Outside, in the courtyard, a chill wind scudded the browning leaves and a fire had been lit in the hearth to offset the damp creeping through the stone walls.

'I hear someone coming,' Anne said, lifting her braided head.

'Nonsense! You couldn't possibly — ,' her mother said impatiently, but Anne repeated stubbornly,

'I can, Mother! I can hear bad news coming. I can hear it plainly.'

'For the love of heaven, child, don't

say such weird things.' The Countess crossed herself hastily and rose, smoothing her gown with nervous fingers. The girl had a queer, dreaming look on her face that made her mother feel positively threatened.

They could all hear the trotting of hooves now and loud voices and then the Earl, booted and spurred, with a dust-stained cloak still hanging from his shoulders, strode in, his hawk face scarlet with tiredness and temper.

'Before God, what ails you?' the Countess demanded in alarm, omitting the customary greeting.

'Edward is married!' the Earl said shortly.

'The King? He and the Lady Bona — ,' she began, puzzled.

'Not the Lady Bona!' he interrupted fiercely. 'Dame Grey. Edward has married Dame Grey. Flouted the French alliance, deceived his entire Council and last May secretly wed Dame Elizabeth Grey! He did not see fit to inform any of us until now.'

'It's unbelievable! She's widowed already and has two children!' his wife exclaimed.

'She has a pack of relatives,' the Earl said gloomily. 'The Court is now infested with Woodvilles and Greys, all looking for coin and position! It makes me look a complete fool! All my efforts to bring about the marriage with Lady Bona set at nought because a low-born widow flutters her eyelashes at my handsome cousin King!'

'Her mother was Duchess of Bedford,' the Countess said, with an air of trying to be fair.

'And her father was plain Richard Woodville, Knight!' he retorted. 'Her first husband was a small landowner of no account, and none of her sisters are wed!'

'Oh dear!' The Countess sat down abruptly and stared at her husband in dismay.

'I think Edward has been bewitched,' he said, pulling off his cloak and flinging it over a stool. 'To take her as a mistress would have been very right and proper, but the clever bitch held out for marriage.'

'Can it not be set aside?'

'On what grounds? Her first husband is safely dead and Edward may marry where he chooses. Oh, it is perfectly legal! But to do it in this fashion, without my advice! It is the ingratitude of it all that spikes me to the heart. My cousin owes his crown to me but now that it is safely on his head he behaves as he pleases. I am disappointed in him, deeply disappointed!'

'You have not yet quarrelled with him openly?' she inquired in alarm.

'Indeed not! I could not avoid expressing my surprise at the high-handed manner in which he had behaved, but I undertook to welcome her into the family and to honour her as Queen.'

'Queen!' The Countess almost spat the word.

'It has undermined my position.' The Earl poured himself a beaker of wine and drank it angrily, his hand shaking a little. 'It has greatly undermined my position! I made that known to His Grace. Privately, of course, for I'd not have open quarrel between us. I made it clear that I was hurt — deeply hurt at his lack of confidence in me! Deeply hurt!'

'I am not expected to bow the knee to the Woodville woman, am I?' she demanded.

'We must all bow the knee. You hear that, girls?' He swung round upon his open-mouthed daughters. 'The King has been wed these four months to a lady who is now true Queen of the realm.'

'By marriage but not by birth,' their mother reminded them. 'This will cause a tremendous scandal. Why, it was as bad when Henry V's widow went off and married that low-born Welsh squire — worse, for Katherine de Valois was not a ruling monarch but a mere dowager queen, and Edward is the King.'

'She's a very pretty woman,' the Earl said, calming down a trifle. 'One has to admire her looks. Edward is head over heels in love with her.'

'Love! What has love to do with getting married?' the Countess asked in astonishment. 'Edward is a Plantagenet, not a peasant! His marriage is important to the realm, vital to the realm. He was bound by gratitude to consult you and take your advice on such a matter! I am inclined to think there must be witchcraft in it. There is no possibility — ?'

'None at all. The lady is a respectable Christian,' the Earl said. 'She has swarms of kinsfolk too, all of them winging their way to Court as greedily as wasps to a honey-pot. They will grab everything they can get. Already the King has settled 4,000 marks a year on his bride, and bestowed upon her the manors of Greenwich and Shene, and a private house in London too.'

'And the crown matrimonial,' the

Countess reminded him. 'Husband, what are we going to do?'

'At the moment there is nothing we can do save accept the situation, but we will talk further. I am deeply disappointed in Edward, deeply disappointed!'

'He has shown himself ungrateful,' the Countess said, her face flushing as deeply as her lord's. 'Ingratitude in a King can never be condoned.'

'So we bite our tongues!' the Earl warned. 'We say nothing, nothing in public. You heard that, girls?'

He swung round again upon his daughters, frowning at them both. Isobel nodded her head wisely, but Anne ventured to inquire.

'Will the Duke of Gloucester be returning to us now?'

'No, chuck.' Her father's face softened a little. 'He is ordered to remain at Court and complete his education there. The King has a great fondness for his youngest brother. The Woodvilles will seek to oust both him and the

Duke of Clarence from Edward's favour, so it is important that both George and Richard remain at Court, near to His Grace's person for the moment. But I've no doubt both will visit us again before long.'

'And what of the French alliance?' the Countess asked.

'I will go personally to France and salvage what I can,' he said. 'The King may not care about his foreign policy, but I have a reputation to maintain. My own credibility is threatened by my cousin's high-handed actions. The Woodvilles have no influence save what they can filch from the King. The Nevilles make monarchs and we shall see how long Edward Plantagenet can sit upon his throne without my support!'

'You'll not abandon his Grace? I am very fond of Edward!' the Countess said in alarm.

'And I am devoted to him,' the Earl said sombrely. 'He will realise the depth of my devotion when he wakes from his

dream of passion and finds Woodvilles
running all over the place! He will learn
his errors then and seek my help. He
will learn that I am not named
'Kingmaker' for nothing!'

3

At last she had a gown with a train and a butterfly hennin beneath which all her hair was tucked. It was a beautiful dress, Anne thought, admiring herself in the long glass. Of deep peach silk, embroidered with gold and silver daisies, its shallow neck was outlined with white fur, its sleeves long and tight, its high waistline marked by a broad belt of rose velvet. Her hennin was covered with gold and silver gauze, and about her neck was clasped a chain of gold and silver links with rubies between them.

'You are ten years old now and must begin to take your rightful place in society,' the Countess had said.

Anne wondered sometimes where her rightful place was. She was no longer a child to be indulged and scolded, and she was not yet a woman grown to be allowed some voice in her own destiny. And she had not yet been taken to Court.

The occasion for the new dress was the enthronement of her uncle, George Neville, as Archbishop of York. The very fact that he had been appointed proved, to their own satisfaction at least, that Neville influence was as powerful as ever. In the north their sway was still undisputed and the low-born Woodvilles regarded as upstarts who sought to ween the handsome young King from his loyal adherents.

It had been a splendid ceremony for which the Countess and her daughters had ridden to York and were lodged now at the Bishop's Palace. Anne was fond of her uncle, who spoke gently to her on those rare occasions when they met, but she was in awe of her other Neville uncle, John of Northumberland, who prided himself on his blunt speaking. Duke John called her 'shrimp', and swung her into the air as if she were two years old. He was convinced that children adored him, and would have been deeply hurt to learn that one niece did everything in her power to keep out of the way whenever he was expected.

Fortunately, he was too much involved in the arranging of the ceremonies to have any leisure to spare for the smaller members of his clan, and Anne had enjoyed herself tremendously as she watched the procession of churchmen and knights wend their way through the narrow streets towards the Minister.

Now they were all taking their places at small tables set out in the high-raftered hall. The banquet itself had been bought by the Earl and bade fair to rival any banquet that the Woodville's might care to give. Joints of pork, beef, lamb, veal and venison had been roasted to crackling perfection, and the sweet dishes were of elaborate magnificence, red and green jelly dragons, angels of marchpane with wings of spun sugar, pastries thick with crab apple, damson and greengage, jugs of cream yellow as butter, vats of ale and malmsey and hippocras. Each dish was brought in to the accompaniment of music and dancing, and everywhere fluttered the banners of the Nevilles, the bear holding a ragged staff.

The splendour was exciting enough, but her heart had jumped into her throat when she beheld Richard, small and slim, among the crowd of nobles. He was more grandly dressed than she had ever seen him, in an overtunic of coral velvet spangled with gold and edged with white fur, over a long sleeved tunic of russet brown and hose of mushroom pink. In other respects he had not altered save to grow a couple of inches in the two years since they had met. His hair fell lankly to his shoulders and his dark eyes lit up as he spotted her.

'Anne! God give you greeting!' He bowed over her hand and took a seat next to her without waiting to be asked.

'God give you greeting, sir.' Her cheeks flushed with the excitement of the meeting and the room blurred a little.

'My sister Elizabeth is with me.' He indicated a tall, slim young woman who gave a vague, gentle inclination of the head. Elizabeth was Duchess of Suffolk and had a small son called John, Anne remembered having heard. Perhaps she was thinking of her little boy now and wishing she could be at home with him.

'Lady Elizabeth.' Anne nodded her own head cautiously, for she was not yet accustomed to the weight of her headdress.

'It is so long since we met,' Richard was saying under cover of the general conversation.

'More than two years,' she agreed. 'We hoped that you would have come north before this time.'

'My time is not my own,' he said. 'I am required to attend His Grace when I am not at my studies, but I have thought often of my happy months at Middleham.'

'We must petition His Grace to release you to us more frequently,' the Countess said, leaning across to smile at the Duke. 'It would be too sad if you were persuaded to neglect old friends. We see something of dear George from time to time, but your company is sadly missed.'

'Not at my wish,' Richard said, resentment creeping into his voice. 'Since the Queen bore a child we are all required to wait upon her almost constantly.'

'A princess, is it not? Named for her mother. Too charming,' the Countess said, flicking her fingers as if she were brushing away a fly.

'Yes. A girl, madam. His Grace hopes for a son next time, but he dotes upon the Lady Bess.'

'Charming!' the Countess said again, her tone dismissing a mere Woodville princess.

'Will you be returning to Middleham

with us?' Anne asked hopefully.

He shook his dark head, his eyes regretful.

'I am due to return south when this banquet is over. We are leaving at dawn.'

Disappointment gripped her. An hour or two, in the midst of company, was all that they had. They met so seldom and there was so much she wanted to ask him. Were the Woodvilles as greedy and arrogant as people said? His face in repose had a wary, guarded expression that hinted at loneliness. Perhaps the Queen and her relatives despised him for his youth and his small size. She looked at him in sudden, fierce protectiveness.

Later, while an interval between courses was being filled up by the tumbling of some gypsies, he leaned towards her and said, his voice low, 'You know that your father plans to wed Isobel to my brother of Clarence?'

'I thought it was almost certain,' she said.

'The King has forbidden it,' Richard said. 'He has told George privately that he must look elsewhere for a bride.'

'But why?' she asked in bewilderment.

'The Woodvilles are not willing to have a Neville so greatly matched,' Richard said.

'What is it to do with them?' she enquired.

'The King married a Woodville,' Richard reminded her, 'and the whole family have sought to influence him so that only they make the best marriages and seize the greatest titles.'

'My lady mother has told me of it,' Anne said.

The Countess had raged about it in the privacy of Middleham.

'Richard Woodville jumped up from a plain knight to Earl Rivers and Lord Treasurer, simply because his daughter is made Queen! Her brother Anthony made Governor of the Isle of Wight! Six of her sisters married off to peers of the realm! It is past all reason!'

'His Grace is hedged about with Woodvilles,' Richard said now, 'and the rest of us are scratched to death on the thorns!'

'Isobel will be so disappointed,' Anne mourned softly. 'She wishes to marry the Duke of Clarence very much.'

'The King is talking about marrying George off to Mary of Burgundy,' Richard said. 'She is a very great heiress, and her father, who is a widower these six months, has offered for my sister Margaret. She is 20 years old and still unwed.'

'So Lady Margaret would become her own brother's mother-in-law!' Anne stifled a reluctant giggle.

'Your father has not spoke to you formally of your own betrothal?'

She shook her head, her eyes on the dancers.

'We are both considered too unimportant, I suppose,' he said, the resentment creeping back into his voice. 'I have always thought that George would marry Isobel and that you and I would marry.' He said it so calmly and casually. Anne, a spoon dug into her jelly, gazed at him. 'Now we must wait,' he said, in the same considering tone. 'If I asked His Grace to allow me to wed you he would be persuaded against it by the Woodvilles. We must be patient and wait.'

She was silent, her eyes darkly shining, and he touched her fingers with his own and said,

'Will you wait, Lady Anne? Will you?'

'Yes, of course,' she breathed, and thought it strange that he should even need to ask.

The dancers were finishing their act with a series of cartwheels, slender limbs flashing under their spangled garments. Like wheels turning. Like years passing. She was ten years old and had known Richard for half her life. The thought sobered her.

'We'll speak again,' Richard said, giving her a little nod, laying one finger along his lips in token of a secret.

She put her own finger to her lips

and dug into her jelly again. Around her the conversation flowed pleasantly and Lady Elizabeth smiled her kind, vague smile.

The Duke, attended by his retainers, left the celebrations before they ended in preparation for his early start the next day, and Anne lost interest in the proceedings and sat, trying to stifle her yawns, as the loyal toasts were drunk and the long speeches of acclamation began.

They stayed in York for nearly a week, the Countess taking advantage of her holiday to buy gowns, slippers and riding saddles for herself and two daughters. Isobel, being the elder, had the more costly and elaborate garments, but both girls returned to the fastness of Middleham with their packages bulging with new clothes and more luggage piled high on the carts that brought up the rear of their train.

There was to be a splendid tournament at Smithfield that promised to be one of the wonders of the age, and

Anne would have liked to see it, but her mother said that no ladies were attending and that, with the Woodvilles arranging it, the whole affair was bound to be vulgar. The Earl would certainly not be attending, as he was journeying to and fro on his own diplomatic business.

'Edward may press for the Burgundian alliance, but I shall work for the French treaty,' he informed his assembled family. 'My royal cousin thinks he can flout all our wishes and please the Woodvilles, but he will learn that the name of Neville is still foremost in the realm!'

Anne, listening from her seat in the corner, thought with a sudden flash of insight,

'My father wishes Edward to rule England for as long as my father rules Edward.'

The thought savoured of disloyalty, and she thrust it aside, smiling dutifully as her uncle, John of Northumberland, tweaked her cheek in passing, roaring that she was as white as a bled cock and ought to eat more meat.

At Middleham news came slowly and, for much of the winter, the roads were closed by snow and ice. She wished that she and Richard had made some arrangement to send letters, but to do that would be to risk their secret being found out. Of one thing she was certain. Richard had said that one day they would be wed and she knew that it would happen.

Meanwhile the King's Woodville Queen had a second daughter who was called Mary in honour of the Virgin. The male heir was as far off as ever, which helped in some measure to alleviate the fury of the Earl over the fact that all his careful diplomatic work had gone for nothing. The King's sister, Margaret, was to wed Charles of Burgundy after all. The Earl personally escorted the bride to the quayside at Margate on the first stage of her wedding journey, and returned to Middleham briefly to declare that his jaw ached from baring his teeth at the Woodvilles.

Isobel asked eagerly about George of Clarence and was assured that he was well and as set on marriage with her as ever.

'He has the greatest affection for you, my dear, and he reposes absolute trust in my judgment. The Queen and her kinsfolk have done everything in their power to cut out George and Richard, but I have never wavered in my kind intentions towards them both,' her father said, patting her shoulder.

Anne longed to ask if he had any thought of her marriage, but she kept silent, bending her dark head over her sewing, thinking of the little Duke being reared far away in the south.

'There is great discontent in the land,' the Earl was saying, stretching his long legs before the fire. 'People say my royal cousin spends all his time in feasting and pleasure, and has no time for his old allies.'

'There are risings in Wales,' John of

Northumberland said. 'The Tudors still declare they have a right to the throne.'

'Welsh upstarts!' The Earl swung his feet to the floor and glowered at his brother. 'Woodville upstarts! God give me patience! My cousin will lose all while he pussyfoots it with his queen! I tell you, brother, the way is being cleared for Queen Margaret to return and set her witless spouse upon the throne again!'

'Then it is our duty to stand by Edward,' John of Northumberland said.

'Have I ever done anything else?' the Earl demanded. 'I have given him the best advice any man could have, spent thousands in his service! He owes his throne to me, as I am always telling him.'

Perhaps her father told the King too often, Anne thought. Perhaps His Grace was fond of the Woodvilles because they had nothing save what he had granted them. She wished she dared say as much, but young girls were expected to sit mutely while state affairs were being discussed.

The Countess was being far from mute. Her clear voice rated them all. 'Talk is the last word of the impotent! There was a time when you would both have acted! The King is young — '

'Twenty-six or seven, and father of two princesses,' John interposed.

'In the head,' she continued as if he had not spoken. 'He is under the spell of these Woodvilles, subject to bad influences, and for his own sake he must be protected.'

'I will bid you good morrow,' John said, rising with more haste than grace.

'Going so soon?' his brother asked in surprise.

'When the conversation tends towards treason it is my turn to leave. Madam, I beg you have a care!'

He bowed and strode out, calling for his horse.

'A broken reed!' the Countess said, staring after him. 'I always said that he would not have the wit to move when occasion offered! I hope he has no thoughts of tittle-tattle.'

'John will say nothing,' the Earl said.

'And you will do nothing, is that it?' Her blue eyes blazed at him. 'Your diplomacy is failed, your advice ignored, your influence set at nought, and you sit! Our daughter is not considered good enough now for the King's brother, though the Woodvilles marry the highest in the land with impunity! And what of Gloucester? Time was when Edward was glad to have his young brother reared here! Now he is pulled in the wake of the Woodvilles.'

'I have spoken to Richard,' the Earl cut her short.

Anne's needle was poised above the silk.

'And what does he say?' the Countess asked eagerly.

'That he dislikes the Woodvilles as much as we do, and loves his brother of Clarence, wishing him well in his suit to Isobel.'

'So we have Richard,' she said.

'And that he loves his brother the King, and will do nothing without his knowledge and consent. He reminded me of his motto, 'Loyalty binds me', and said that he would live by it.'

'The young puppy!' the Countess exclaimed.

'Ah, well, he's scarce 16 and has no standing army,' the Earl excused. 'It is milord of Clarence who is of greater account.'

'Not to me,' Anne thought in desolation. 'Not to me.'

'There is a rising threatened in Yorkshire,' the Earl said. 'In a month or two it may become necessary for me to call up my levies.'

'So!' The Countess drew a long breath and smiled at her husband. 'And what must I do, my lord?'

'Tell Isobel to make ready for a journey.'

'A journey? To where?' she demanded.

'I am taking Isobel to Calais,' the

Earl said. 'You see the point of it, my dear?'

'Indeed you make it very clear,' the Countess murmured.

They exchanged glances of complete understanding.

Anne put down her sewing and slipped from the room. So Isobel was to travel to Calais. She wondered what was afoot.

Her uncle was swearing at his squire as he mounted up in the courtyard, but he turned as she appeared at the foot of the steps.

'So it's you, shrimp! What ails you?'

'Nothing, sir.' She went across to him timidly, her dark eyes raised to his face. 'Do you ride now to join the King?'

'I am a loyal subject,' he said curtly.

'So is my lord father,' she said quickly. 'He wants only what is best for the realm.'

'As you say, girl.' He looked down at her with sudden pity and said, 'How old are you, mammet?'

'Close on 13, uncle.'

'You look younger,' he said abruptly. 'Don't let them spoil you, girl. Court life is a great way of ageing a body quickly.'

'Will you be seeing the Duke?' she found courage to ask.

'Which one? George of Clarence is at Calais.'

'Gloucester,' she said. 'Will you be seeing the Duke of Gloucester?'

'I expect so. He will be in His Grace's train. Why?'

'Would you tell him that I have not forgotten?' she asked.

'Forgotten what?'

'Oh, just that. Will you, uncle?'

'Aye. Aye, I'll do it!' he said. 'Now give us a kiss, niece, and keep that little nose of yours out of treasons!'

The word had such an ugly ring. She watched him swing to the saddle and ride out with his squire at his heels.

'Am I to travel to Calais too?' she inquired of her mother the next day.

'To Calais? What put that into your head?' the Countess demanded.

'My lord father is taking Isobel. You were speaking of it.'

'I had forgotten you were here.' The Countess frowned and then decided to confide in her younger child. 'You know that your father is the King's most faithful servant?'

'Yes, madam.'

'And that the King, influenced by the Woodvilles, ignores your father's counsel and has signed a treaty with Burgundy instead of France?'

'Yes, madam.'

'Your father plans to wed Isobel to the Duke of Clarence. If tidings of it were to leak out the Woodvilles would prevent it, so they will be wed secretly in Calais. Your uncle, the Archbishop, has obtained a dispensation for the match as George and Isobel are within the forbidden degrees of kinship.'

'There was talk of a rising,' Anne prompted.

'There are always risings,' her mother said vaguely. 'Your father may be forced to raise his troops and rescue the King from his present difficulties.'

'Perhaps His Grace doesn't wish to be rescued,' Anne dared to say.

'It is the good of the realm that must be considered,' the Countess said.

And that meant the good of the Nevilles, Anne thought. She wondered, with a new touch of cynicism, who would be behind the northern rising.

Isobel was choosing garments for the journey and looked solemnly important as she went about her tasks. She was prettier than ever, Anne thought, with her fair hair and skin, blue eyes, and tall, graceful figure. Within a week or two she would be Duchess of Clarence, married to the young man of her choice. If Richard had agreed to stand with the Earl, there might have been two weddings at Calais, Anne thought wistfully, but Richard, though he disliked the Woodvilles, would do nothing behind His Grace's back. Anne admired him for that even if it did make her time of waiting longer. She sometimes repeated to herself the words, 'Loyalty binds me', and decided they applied equally to herself.

Her father and sister rode out with a small company, all trying to look as if they were making a local visit somewhere or other. In fact it was doubtful if the King would hear anything of their journey until they were back in Yorkshire with Isobel and George safely married, but there was no harm in taking precautions. The Countess, having watched them ride out, turned back into the Great Hall with a feeling of satisfaction. At 16 Isobel was quite ready to consummate the marriage, and George was, from all appearences, a lusty young man. It would be rather pleasant to have grandchildren. The Woodville Queen had just presented the King with a third daughter. She was certainly proving prolific even if the male heir had not yet been born.

'If His Grace died without issue,' she mused aloud. 'It is in the highest degree unlikely that any of the little princesses would be accepted as monarch. George of Clarence would be next in line.'

Handsome George, devoted to his cousin Warwick, and married to Isobel. A smile curved the Countess's handsome mouth. It was not outside the bounds of possibility that her elder daughter might one day wear the crown. She wished no harm to Edward, of course, but there was no denying that life was uncertain at the best of times. The summer brought plague and the winter brought the coughing sickness, and there were the intermittent hazards of battle. It was a miracle, the Countess thought piously, that anybody ever survived.

She went through into the family solar where Anne was conning her book, and stood for a few minutes gazing thoughtfully at her younger daughter. The girl was no beauty. She was too small and pale, and she lacked the sparkle that might have made people forget her physical deficiencies, but she was a good, obedient girl and she would make a very charming

Duchess of Gloucester, if only Richard could be drawn away from the King and made to understand that his best friends were his Neville cousins.

Anne, looking up said,

'Did you wish me to attend you, Mother?'

'No, no. Finish your tale. Is it an interesting one?' The Countess glanced at the ornate cover.

' 'The Dialogues of Plato'.' Anne's sallow little face brightened. 'The Archbishop lent it to me.'

'The Dialogues of Plato', forsooth! The Countess gave her daughter a smile, murmured 'Charming' and passed on.

4

'Anne, are ye abed yet?'

The voice of the Countess, although it was pitched low, throbbed with excitement.

'No, madam. I am awake.' Anne, who had been lying fully dressed on her pallet, rose at once, smoothing down her skirt. At any other time she would have been scolded for her sluttishness, but her mother had other matters on her mind.

'A messenger has come,' she said, closing the door and standing with her back against it. 'You father will be here in an hour.'

'Is he well?' Anne asked anxiously.

'Well and in high spirits,' her mother declared. 'The Duke of Clarence is with him, which will please Isobel, for the poor girl has moped ever since George rode away.'

That had been only a few days after the return of the newlyweds from Calais. Isobel had taken to married life with alacrity, and was not in the least pleased to have her splendid young mate gallop off with the Earl to put down the rebels.

'The King and Gloucester have come with them,' the Countess said. 'His Grace is rescued from the Woodvilles and in the protective custody of your father.'

'A prisoner?' Anne stared in bewilderment.

'Acting under advice,' the Countess said carefully. 'He has been brought north for his own safety.'

'Oh.' Anne spoke blankly, puzzled as to how a rebellion against the King could turn into a triumph for the Earl when he had gone to support Edward.

'The Woodville Queen's father and her brothers have been executed,' the Countess said.

'But they were not rebels against the King!' Anne exclaimed.

'They were bad advisers to his Grace,' her mother said firmly. 'Your father was certain, from information received, that they were contemplating treason.'

'Oh.' Anne said again.

'The country is in uproar,' the Countess announced with a certain amount of grim satisfaction. 'There are dangers everywhere, save here in the north, which is strong for your father.'

'I cannot understand,' Anne ventured, 'how it comes about that my lord father and the Duke of Clarence ride out to fight rebels and come back with the King as prisoner.'

'In protective custody,' the Countess said. 'The power of the Woodvilles must be smashed so that the King may govern as he chooses.'

'Or as my father chooses,' Anne muttered, wrapping a cloak about herself and following her mother out to the draughty gallery.

'Your father knows what is best for the realm,' the Countess said. 'His

Grace has been led astray by bad counsel, and matters must be set right. He will be lodged here while the country is brought under some measure of control.'

People, Anne seemed to remember, had spoken in the same way about King Henry, and now he was a prisoner, and his wife and son were in exile. She trailed, in some perplexity, after her mother, who was loudly calling for candles and some hot food to be made ready.

They streamed over the drawbridge, the autumn wind catching the flames of their pitch-soaked torches and sending them flaring backwards. Anne, standing nervously by her mother and Isobel, wondered how one was supposed to greet a King who had unexpectedly become a prisoner. Even in her inexperience she knew that 'protective custody' was a phrase that meant nothing at all. He who held the person of the King was ruler of England.

'My lady wife!' The Earl was first to

alight and embrace her warmly. 'We have an unexpected guest.'

'But none the less welcome, Sire,' the Countess said. 'We are greatly relieved to see you after your recent dangers.'

'Most kind of you, cousin.' The King had dismounted and was kissing her on both cheeks. 'Your husband has been most assiduous on my behalf ever since I came into the north. Indeed I was not aware of the extent of my dangers until he rescued me from them. I hope you have something for a famished traveller, for I swear my stomach cleaves to my backbone!'

'A simple repast, sir. You remember my daughters?'

'Indeed I do.' Edward, who didn't seem to realise that he was a prisoner, beamed at them both. 'I owe you a wedding gift, my dear Isobel, but it will have to wait a little while. Richard, come and greet your cousins, lad.'

The slight figure, grown since she had seen him but still dwarfed by his brothers, approached and bowed. In the torchlight the young face was a pattern of dark hollows and colourless planes, the eyes cold blackness.

'Shall we go indoors?' Edward threw his arms about the Earl's neck. 'This Yorkshire air is more bracing than I remember, but we in the south grow soft! Cousin Countess, there is a maid in our train who is near her time but would insist on riding with us. Can she be tended?'

'I will have her bedded at once,' the Countess said.

She, too, sounded bewildered, vainly trying to catch her husband's eye as they went into the hall. Isobel had greeted George of Clarence with obvious delight and the King, releasing the Earl from his bear-hug, was gulping at spiced ale.

'It's a welcome respite to be at Middleham again,' he said cordially, wiping his mouth. 'It will afford us an opportunity to talk in peace, my cousin of Warwick. One hears such rumours! Why, milord Pembroke, God rest his soul! was under the impression that you and my brother of Clarence had stirred up the rebellion yourselves in order to discredit my government.'

'A foul slander, Sire, for which he paid,' the Earl said.

'Aye, you beheaded him, did you not? the Earl of Devon, too?'

'He was marching to join Pembroke,' the Earl said.

'Being under the same misapprehension, no doubt?' Edward sighed gently and drank his wine.

'Your Grace has been most badly advised. The Burgundian alliance — '

'Let us not argue politics, cousin,' the King interrupted. 'I can smell the most succulent aroma which leads me to hope food is wafting towards us. Afterwards I think a good night's sleep is indicated before we discuss serious matters. Richard, come and sit with me. Cousin, we owe your good wife an apology for arriving with so little warning! I trust you have not put yourselves out by yielding your bedchamber to me? I shall be quite happy in a guest chamber.'

He spoke with the utmost cordiality, eating his supper with relish, complimenting Isobel on her bridal bloom. Anne watched him, her own eyes puzzled. The King seemed not to care that his father-in-law and brother-in-law had lost their heads, and that he was in Warwick's power. Her gaze moved to Richard, who sat eating in silence. With a little pang she realised that he had not once looked in her direction.

'We only want what is best for Your Grace,' the Earl said.

'As I have informed those who declare that you seek power for your own ends,' Edward assured him. 'No doubt you feared I would be angry at word of the marriage.'

'Which Your Grace forbade,' George reminded him.

'Policy,' the King said blandly, 'is often dictated by necessity. I have a certain fondness for love matches, however, so will not rant too loudly at your disobedience, my dear brother. Isobel is so lovely that I've half a mind to snaffle her myself, but the Pope frowns upon incest!'

'Your Grace's prowess with the ladies is well known,' the Earl bowed.

'And young Richard there is beginning to appreciate their charms,' the King smiled. 'That little lass who rode with us from Warwickshire carries his seed and will give birth to a babe in a day or two.'

It was not true. Richard had vowed to wait for her. He was not yet 17 and that was too young to beget a bastard. The sentences flashed through Anne's mind, scorching her brain like shafts of lightning.

'Who is the girl?' the Countess enquired.

'One of my sister Margaret's sewing maids,' Edward said. 'Fifteen years old and as pretty as a peach. She has no family so Richard took her under his wing.'

It was not true. Richard would never lie with a sewing maid. He would never lie with any maid because he had vowed to wait.

'I will tend her myself,' the Countess said, being proud of her nursing skill. 'I must confess I am astonished you brought her with you. She might have given birth on the road, but there, men never think of such things!'

'Molly insisted,' Richard said, speaking for the first time since they had entered the hall.

It was true. Richard had lain with a sewing maid called Molly and now she was at Middleham about to bear his child. Nothing in the world was safe any longer.

Anne slipped out of the hall and fled to her bedchamber. She was too numb to weep, too angry to rage. For a long time she sat on her bed, arms clasped about her to contain the pain, and when someone tapped on the door she had to swallow hard before she could raise her voice sufficiently to bid them enter.

Richard came in, closing the door behind him. For a moment she stared at him wordlessly and then she sprang up, her voice shaking, her fists clenched.

'How dare you walk into my bedchamber!'

'The others are still at their meal,' he said. 'I wished to talk to you, Anne.'

'To explain about the sewing maid? You need not trouble,' she gasped out.

'Molly is a sweet girl,' he said.

'You evidently found her so!'

'It's lonely at Court,' he said simply. 'I am kept at my books most of the time or in attendance on the Woodville Queen. Oh, Edward is kind to me. God knows that I couldn't wish for a better brother, but he is often away or occupied with affairs of state. Molly has no family and her life has been a hard one. We fell into conversation.'

'And thence into bed, I suppose?' she gibed.

'Many men sire bastards,' he said.

'And you wanted to prove yourself a man? Why? What need had you to break your promise?'

'I have broken no promise,' he said stiffly.

'You vowed to wait for me,' she said miserably.

'And I am waiting! I will wait!' He stepped forward and took her hands in his own firm clasp. 'You cannot think that Molly has anything to do with you and me? Why, she is just a girl who pleasured me for a while when I was feeling miserable!'

'Then why bring her here?' she questioned. 'Why let her ride with you?'

'Because she would not be left behind,' he said. 'Our Molly has a will of her own.'

'*Your* Molly! I'll have no share in the wench!'

'You and I have always been one,' he answered gravely. 'Ever since I first came here I have known that you and I belonged together, that if we were patient we would one day be able to wed. Molly has nothing to hope for from me, so you have no cause to be jealous.'

'I am not in the least jealous,' she said promptly. 'I know that men need their pleasures.'

'And with pleasure comes responsibility. I shall acknowledge the babe as my own and settle an allowance upon Molly. It is the honourable course.'

'I suppose so.' She spoke reluctantly.

'You need not fear,' he said. 'I intend to marry you, Anne.'

'We could have been wed when Isobel and George were,' she reproached.

'That would have meant defying the King, and my first loyalty must be to him,' Richard said.

'But His Grace is here now and my father's star rises again.'

'Stars can set,' he said, and gripped her hands more tightly, his voice low and urgent. 'My cousin of Warwick rides high and the Woodvilles are set down, but Edward is our King. You and I must keep faith with each other and with him.'

'And the girl? What of the girl?'

'When Molly has had her babe they can settle in York,' he said. 'I have sufficient gold to lease a small house for her there. She must not suffer because of her generosity to me.'

It meant no more to him than that! Anne stared at him, aware of the gulf that lay between men's and women's thinking. To Richard the child was merely proof of his manhood and the mother a pleasant diversion.

'If you and I were wed,' she said, 'we could have babes too.'

'When you are older,' he said, 'we will be wed with the King's permission and have fine babes.'

He was not yet 17, but he seemed years older than that. She loosed her hands and tried to match his dignity.

'Then we still wait and keep silent? Sometimes I grow impatient.'

'So do I.' His rare smile embraced

her. 'But I bide my time, Anne. I bide my time.'

He bowed and quietly withdrew before she could answer. She wondered if he had gone to find out if the girl Molly was comfortably bedded and then hated herself for being so untrusting. Richard had promised her that they would marry one day, and she would cling to that and put out of her mind the picture of Richard with his arms about a girl called Molly.

The next morning when she went into the chapel for Mass she saw that the King occupied the best chair with a canopy of state over it, and that he seemed as content as before to be a prisoner. The Earl was evidently on the best of terms with his royal captive. The two ate their breakfast beef from the same dish and Edward's hearty laughter rang out from time to time, drowning any attempt at serious conversation.

George of Clarence had not improved since his marriage, Anne thought critically. He was near as handsome as the King, but he had a petulant mouth and his voice was complaining. Isobel hung on his every word, constantly touching his hand and patting his sleeve as if to reassure herself that he was there. The King, nodding towards them, had said, his voice amused,

'Love matches will become all the rage soon.'

Anne darted a glance at Richard, but he was stolidly eating his breakfast.

It was impossible to settle to her books that day or during the days that followed. She had not inquired in which part of the castle Molly had been lodged, and she hoped that Richard hadn't bothered either. On the rare occasions she saw him he was shooting at the butts or strolling in the courtyard with one or other of the squires. The King, too, seemed perfectly at his ease, playing chess with the Earl, sorting embroidery silks for the Countess, toasting the newlyweds with as much cheerfulness as if he had arranged the marriage himself.

The family were still scattered about the Great Hall, the King chatting to Richard by the door, George and Isobel whispering together in a corner. The Earl and Countess sat at a trestle-table, with Anne on a stool at her mother's knee. She sat very still, her eyes lowered to the book she wasn't troubling to read. An hour before the servant had brought word that Molly had given birth to a daughter.

'A healthy lass!' Edward had exclaimed. 'Congratulations, little brother!'

There had been some good-natured teasing between the three royal brothers, and Richard had gone off to look at the baby, his face a mixture of pleasure and embarrassment.

Sooner or later Anne would be required to admire the child, but for the moment she was spared. The mother must rest and a name be chosen before she would be required to look at the result of Molly's generosity.

'We cannot keep His Grace here for

ever,' the Countess objected.

'We must net the rest of the Woodvilles first,' her husband said. 'And there must be a Proclamation given out to the effect that His Grace reposes the deepest trust in my judgment.'

'Will he sign such a Proclamation?'

'He is ready to sign anything to prove our continued friendship,' the Earl said.

Anne sighed, her head drooping lower. Everyone, it seemed, was happy except herself, and she was only unhappy because she had no patience. That was a virtue she would strive to cultivate.

'Katherine!' the King called suddenly. 'What d'ye think of that for a name?'

'A good one,' the Earl responded, rising and strolling across to join them.

'I was hoping that the Archbishop would agree to baptise the child,' Richard said.

'He's at York. You cannot expect him to leave his palace and interrupt his business to baptise your bastard,' the King said.

'I think that my brother of York would be happy to come,' the Earl said, watching the disappointment on the Duke's face.

'I could ride over and ask him,' Richard said. 'It's a fine day for a gallop.'

'Richard is never content unless he is riding somewhere on some perfectly useless errand,' the King said.

'My lord, you will stand with me in this, won't you?' Richard appealed.

'I see no harm in the lad's riding to York with a few of the squires,' Warwick said judicially, stroking his chin. 'As long as Your Grace isn't thinking of riding with him?'

'I am relishing your hospitality too greatly, my dear cousin and mentor,' Edward said, putting his arm about the Earl.

Anne had risen and followed her father, hoping that Richard would smile at her or drop a casual word in her direction. He took no notice of her at all, however, and she moved back into the shadows again, her eyes downcast.

'Katherine is a very pretty name,' the Countess said approvingly. 'In a week or two the babe can be taken to York with her mother. Now, that's a good girl you found, my lord of Gloucester.'

'Thank you, madam.' He bowed and went out, the Earl at his heels. A few minutes later the slight figure of the Duke, flanked by the squires, trotted through the arch into the covered way.

'Not that I condone immorality,' the Countess said severely, to nobody in particular, 'but men must prove themselves, I suppose, and it's a pretty babe.'

If they mentioned the wretched infant once more she would scream, Anne decided. She saw that the Earl was returning across the courtyard, and saw the King's handsome face break into a smile as if something had just amused him very much.

The same smile was in evidence the

next day when a breathless herald arrived pell-mell from the northern borders with dispatches in his pouch.

'It seems there is a rebellion in Lancashire,' Edward said, breaking the seals and reading rapidly. 'In favour of King Henry, it appears. I thought they would make a bid, but not so soon! Why, we've scarcely managed to subdue the latest outbreak!'

'We can deal with this too,' the Earl said, stooping over the King's shoulder to scan the message. 'I will call out the levies at once.'

'Oh, nobody will come.' Edward said gently.

'Of course they will!' the Countess exclaimed. 'We will summon the troopers and — '

'They will not come until I have returned to London and there proclaimed that there is danger to my crown. I made those arrangements some weeks ago. It would be so easy for orders to be issued in the name of a monarch who is actually a prisoner,' Edward put in.

'You and I can ride to London together, my liege,' the Earl said quickly. 'Then the commons will be able to see for themselves the accord between us.'

'My dear cousin, the amity between us is well known,' Edward said. 'Why, the speed with which you rushed to offer me shelter at Middleham was quite remarkable. Remarkable! I would be content to idle away my entire winter here, but then the armies would not don armour or pick up their weapons and the riots would spread. I think I must start for London as soon as my councillors arrive.'

'Councillors?' The Earl sat down heavily, his eyes blank.

'I sent word to milord Hastings, to the Earls of Essex and Arundel and to the Dukes of Suffolk and Buckingham. They will be riding here to escort me to London. They should be in York by now.'

'With their retainers?' the Earl asked.

Edward leaned back in his chair and smiled again.

'Oh, I think they will be travelling with considerable escort,' he said. 'I understand that your brother of Northumberland is with them too.'

'And your brother of Gloucester will, no doubt, be joining them at York,' the Earl said, a vein throbbing in his temple.

'After making arrangements for the baptism, of course,' the King nodded.

'Then we must arrange for your journey to London,' the Earl said.

'My dear Warwick, you have been inconvenienced quite sufficiently on my behalf,' Edward said charmingly. 'I will borrow half a dozen of your men and ride out to meet my councillors. Perhaps you and my brother of Clarence would hold yourselves in readiness for when you are summoned — or do you have some other scheme?'

'No scheme could possibly compare with the excellence of your own, Sire,' Warwick said heavily.

'My dear cousin, we are always perfectly agreed,' the King said amiably.

Anne, who sat in her usual seat near to the window, was trembling. Beneath the smiles and the courteous words ran a current of something deadly. She folded her hands together tightly, and thought of Richard riding towards York to join the other lords.

Within the hour the King had left, with a dozen gentlemen at arms. The Earl and Countess stood together watching them ride out, the September sunshine marking the harsh line of Warwick's jaw, the tightness of his wife's mouth.

'Have we lost all?' she asked.

'Lost?' The Earl looked at her. 'My dear, we have not even *begun*! My royal cousin has outwitted us this time, but it won't happen again! Before God, I'll not have my influence set at nought!'

'My brother treats me like a fool,' George of Clarence said, his arm about Isobel as he stood in the shelter of the doorway. 'He sets me at nought, not even troubling to chide me for my marriage! It was always Richard he favoured, even when we were children! Always Richard!'

'Milord of Gloucester is a youngling,' the Earl soothed, his own rage dying. 'He is a good lad, and his devotion to the King has a certain touching charm.'

'We are all of us devoted to the King,' the Countess said.

'So long as he acted like a King,' her husband said. 'He has turned his back now on his own blood-kin and made fools of us all. I am deeply hurt by his attitude. Deeply grieved!'

'You would not find me so ungrateful if you extended your favour to me,' the Duke said eagerly. 'It is a cold Court where Woodvilles reign!'

'They do not reign in my household nor ever shall!' Warwick declared. 'We must confer together, cousin. The times are against us now but the season will change. Edward of England will reap a bitter harvest from this ingratitude!'

Anne no longer wanted any part of

this conversation. It threatened her. The air throbbed with hurt pride and disappointed ambition. She turned and stole quietly away, the brown velvet of her kirtle blending with the stone walls.

Across the courtyard the door of the bakehouse stood open and the fragrant scent of new baked bread drifted out. One of the cooks, seeing her hesitate on the threshold, held out a finger of cinnamon cake.

'For you, milady. You always did fancy my dainties,' the woman said.

'Thank you.' Anne took the cake politely, wondering if a big girl of 13 ought to sneak food from kitchens. To make conversation she observed, 'His Grace has ridden out. We must pray for fine weather.'

'Aye.' The cook plunged red hands into white flour. 'King or no King, bread must be set to rise, milady. Have you seen the little Duke's baby yet? Tis a pretty little soul.'

'I don't like babies much,' Anne said curtly, making for the winding stairs that led up to the old nursery.

The two wide, low ceilinged rooms were clean and bare, rushes swept up, curtains and linens stripped from the beds, and the hearth empty. She touched Ankarette's old chair with a finger and set it rocking, and went through to the inner chamber. From the window seat she could look out over the brown and green and russet of the hills, and down the steep hill to the huddled roofs of the little town below.

She finished her bit of cinnamon cake and went in the echoing emptiness to the table where the toy farm had been set. Some hasty hand had swept the miniature buildings and fences and brightly painted figures into an untidy heap. Anne began to set them out again, carefully dotting the table top with cows, sheep and horses.

Richard had made a battle for her and the pigs had won, but there were no bears on a farm. She picked up a fat, pink pig, its wooden tail carved into a cunning flourish and spoke to it severely,

'I am too old to play with you now. I am waiting for my lord of Gloucester to return.'

The pig stared back at her, its eyes tiny black dots. It was, she thought, as tears filled her eyes and began to roll down her cheeks, an exceedingly sad little pig.

5

They were at Warwick Castle, the largest and most splendid of the Earl's strongholds. It was spring and all about the great, grey stone bulk of the fortress the fields sprang green, the apple-trees showering blossom as the honey-scented breeze caught their slender boughs and tossed them beneath the periwinkle blue sky.

Isobel, in the eighth month of her pregnancy, was in a complaining mood as she sat with her mother in the little solar that overlooked the rose garden.

'It is not fitting that I should be separated from my husband at such a time. There has been no letter from him for weeks!'

'Husbands are not of the slightest use at such a time,' the Countess said firmly, 'and you cannot expect George to spend his days writing letters when he has battles to fight.'

Anne wondered how her mother could speak so calmly when the Earl and the Duke were fighting the King. She was not sure how it had all come about. At Christmas her father and George had gone to Court to reaffirm their loyalty to Edward, and there had been a general reconciliation. And then as the winter snows melted there had come word of a rising in Lincolnshire and trouble in the Welsh Marches. Anne had thought at first that the rising was in favour of King Henry, but it seemed that the rebels wanted to put George of Clarence on the throne and that the entire business had been planned by her father.

'The King is as deeply entangled with the Woodvilles as ever,' her mother had explained. 'We will not have good government until Edward is deposed. He will be kept in close custody after his abdication and then my lord of Clarence can ascend the throne, and the house of Neville will come into its own again.'

Unfortunately Edward showed no signs of allowing himself to be deposed. Instead he had raised his levies, dispatched his brother Gloucester to hold the royal line along the Welsh borders, and ordered his brother Clarence and his cousin Warwick to submit to his rule.

Since then events had been so crowded and confused that Anne had given up trying to understand anything, and ridden south to Warwickshire with only one small consolation.

Her father, seeing her troubled look, had paused during a hurried conversation with the Countess to say kindly,

'When George is safely crowned, my dear, I intend to match you with young Gloucester. You would like that?'

'Yes, oh yes, sir!' Her face had sparkled into delight, and the Countess, glancing at her younger daughter, thought with some surprise that the girl looked quite comely.

'You have my word on it,' the Earl

said, patting Anne's cheek.

Now they sat in the tiny sunlit chamber and waited for news. No doubt Warwickshire would soon rise en masse to sweep its Earl in triumph to London.

'Lord Stanley will rise and march to cut off the advance of Richard's troops,' the Countess said now. 'He owes us that much, being my own sister's husband.'

'My uncle of Northumberland rides with the King,' Anne said.

'John is a fool,' the Countess said, biting off a length of thread. 'And he is no longer Earl of Northumberland. Edward repaid his loyalty by giving the earldom back to Harry Percy. So much for royal gratitude!'

'George will issue a general pardon when the rebels are brought in,' Isobel said, shifting to a more comfortable position.

'But I thought we were the rebels,' Anne began.

'Nonsense!' the Countess said sharply.

'Your lord father wants what is best for the realm. There is nothing rebellious about that!'

'How can we be rebels when George is going to be King?' Isobel inquired.

Anne subsided. At 14 she was still poised uneasily between childhood and womanhood, and when she ventured an opinion it was generally considered to be the wrong one.

'Not that I have anything against Edward,' the Countess said. 'He is a very amiable and charming person, but sadly headstrong! I am certain he was bewitched into that Woodville marriage, but of course one can never prove it.'

'Anne will be Duchess of Gloucester,' Isobel said, smiling at her sister.

'There are riders coming.' Anne, her own sewing laid aside, was at the window, shielding her eyes against the brightness as she peered through the glass.

'Through the rose garden? Don't be so silly!' the Countess began, raising herself to look in the same direction and immediately altering her cry to 'Lord be praised! Your father is come!'

'Is George with him?' Isobel demanded.

'Aye. Wait with your sister, Anne, while I see what's afoot!' The Countess hurried out, the points of her hennin catching on the arras as she went.

'Perhaps I am already Queen?' Isobel said, suddenly hopeful.

'I think not.' Anne's thin little frame was suddenly tense. 'Why would they come to the side gate if the news is good?'

'Girls!' The Countess, spots of colour burning her cheek bones, returned. 'Girls, we must make ready to travel at once.'

'Something went wrong?' Isobel, her own cheeks paling, caught at her mother's sleeve.

'Stanley's own troops were cut off by Gloucester's force,' the Countess said. 'My precious brother-in-law turned around and went home again!'

'But what of the others?' Isobel

demanded. 'Lord Welles and Sir Thomas Dymmock of Lincoln — ?'

'Taken and beheaded. Our own men melting away like snow, and your father and George called 'great rebels'! We must leave at once.'

'Are we going to surrender?' Anne asked, suddenly hopeful.

'Don't be foolish, girl!' her mother snapped, nervously impatient. 'This is a setback, but there is no question of our giving up! We will go to France and seek the aid of King Louis. Your father is on the best of terms with His Grace. The very best of terms!'

'But are we going at once? I am in no fit state to travel,' Isobel said fearfully.

'You could go in a litter,' Anne began, but the Countess interrupted, her voice rising,

'A litter will be too conspicuous and too slow. You will have to mount up with the rest of us.'

'But the child? If I am taken in labour on the way.'

'You are a Neville,' her mother said

firmly. 'Neville women do not give birth to their infants along the road. Anne, go and change your dress, and close your mouth, do! You look half-witted, just standing there.'

Anne fled, passing her father and brother-in-law, who were hastily stuffing down salt beef and bread. It seemed as if everything had turned upside down again and from being sister to a prospective queen she was now the daughter of a rebel.

She afterwards had no clear recollections of that wild journey through the mild springtime. They rode hard for Exeter, pausing only to change mounts and snatch a bite to eat. Anne prided herself on her horsemanship, but hours of galloping bruised the calves of her legs and hurt her wrists. Isobel had been hoisted to her pony and clung there, sobbing as she was jolted up and down, but not even George had leisure to spare for sympathy.

Once or twice they met small groups of men, some with pitchforks over their shoulders, trailing along with no very sensible idea of where they were bound. One man in leather breeches and tunic hailed the Earl, asking in thick country accents, if there was a battle to be fought.

'None, so you may as well turn for home!' the Earl shouted back.

It was strange to ride out unrecognised, without a fluttering banner before her or a pageboy in attendance. There were, apart from themselves, only a dozen gentlemen-at-arms, and she guessed that if they ran into a patrol of the King's or of Richard's it would be impossible to escape. Perhaps it would save a great deal of trouble if they were captured, she thought. Her father and George would be put in the Tower for a few months and Isobel would be able to have her baby in comfort. Once or twice she glanced over her shoulder, half hoping to see Richard galloping after them, but nobody came.

They stopped at a farmhouse once to snatch a few hours sleep, and the woman who kept the place brought them some eggs and ham, and showed the ladies a small chamber in the eaves where they could rest. At close quarters a farm was not quite as attractive as Anne had imagined. The rooms were tiny and there were no tapestries or silver candlesticks or carved furniture, and she suspected the straw was crawling with fleas.

She had scarcely dropped off to sleep when she was being shaken awake again by her mother and hustled down the ladder into the smoky hall, where her father was already pulling on his cloak and swearing at his man-at-arms who was trying to buckle on his lord's sword.

'How is your sister?' he asked, catching Anne's hand in his own as she came near.

'She is more rested, sir, but the ride does her no good.'

'It does none of us any good!' George said violently. 'Why should we take to our heels in this manner?'

'Because we have no army,' the Earl said patiently, giving his son-in-law a barely concealed glance of irritation. 'Because my royal cousin — your brother and your little brother — are both hot on our heels. Because Louis of France can provide us with the soldiers that we need. Is that clear, George?'

'Yes, milord,' the Duke said sulkily.

He did not, Anne thought, sound very much like a prospective King. She turned to help Isobel, who was descending the ladder groaningly, her swollen body scarcely concealed by her voluminous overgown. She was brushed aside by George, rushing to assist his wife, and the Earl gave his chosen monarch another look of ill-suppressed impatience.

It was almost dawn. The farm woman, the gold coins the Earl had given her sweetening her smile, opened the door and sank into a curtsy. She was not absolutely certain who her visitors had been but there was no doubt they were illustrious, though she didn't think much of a husband who dragged his wife out riding when she was at least seven months gone.

They rode on, Isobel drooping more noticeably now, Anne's fingers chafed within her doeskin gloves. The journey was becoming a nightmare and even the Countess had lost her healthy colour and wore a perpetual frown of anxiety.

'We can lodge on the outskirts of the city,' the Earl said, pointing with his whip towards a huddle of houses ahead. 'George and I can buy our passage to Calais. Governor Wenlock will admit us.'

Anne heard his words through a fog of weariness. She ached in every bone and her sympathy for Isobel was dulled by her own discomfort. Wearily she urged her horse along the road, hearing George's voice complaining bitterly that it was against his royal dignity to creep out of the country in such a hole-and-corner manner.

The inn was small and quiet, the landlord a tight-mouthed individual who looked as if he received a number of exhausted members of the nobility every day of his life. If he guessed the identity of any of his guests he said nothing but sent an ostler one way to tend the horses and a maidservant the other to fetch hot water and warm towels for the ladies.

'Will we be able to stay here for a few days?' Isobel asked, hanging on to her husband's hand. 'I feel so bad! Please, may we not stay here for a little while?'

'May we not?' The Duke looked towards the Earl, who shook his head, though his eyes as they rested on his daughter were anxious.

'We must hire a boat at once before word of our being here leaks out,' he said. 'Isobel, you be a good girl and let your mother care for you now. Soon we'll be on board ship, bound for France.'

He nodded at her and, jerking his head at George, went out. The Duke loosed his wife's hand and went after him, as if, thought Anne, the Earl and not he were going to be made King.

'You must eat something before you sleep,' the Countess said to Anne.

'Yes, madam.'

She went obediently over to a table by the window where a selection of cold meats, cheeses and fruit had been set. She was far too tired to taste anything, but she ate obediently, swallowing and chewing, the room blurring before her eyes.

No doubt her father would quickly find a boat and they would sail to France. She was no longer certain what was supposed to happen then, save that George was to be made King, and that the power would be in her father's hands again, and that some time in the distant future she and Richard would be married. It was the only thing to which she could cling, and then even that began to slip away as sleep overcame her, and the last conscious thought in her mind was the slow desolation of hope deferred.

'Anne, wake up!' She was being

shaken out of a dream and her eyelids were too heavy to lift.

The Countess was dressed, or perhaps she had not taken her clothes off at all. Anne struggled to sit up, forcing her eyes open. Isobel was on her feet, George's arm about her shoulders.

'Is the King come?' Anne asked sleepily.

Perhaps if the tall, glowing figure of royal Edward would loom in the doorway everything would change back to what it had been before.

'We've a boat hired,' the Earl said, 'but the King is no more than an hour behind us, so we have to embark at once. We'll make Calais in two days if the wind remains fair.'

They were leaving, and they had scarcely arrived. Anne dragged on her garments, wishing they would forget all about her. The thought came to her that nobody was chasing *her* as a rebel, that she could slip away somewhere and wait until the King arrived. Then her father gave her a swift hug and pushed her gently ahead of him through the door.

They were hurrying through narrow streets that smelled of tar and brine. She stumbled occasionally over the cobblestones, and her father put his arm about her and swept her on in the light of the torches. They made weird, flickering patterns against the walls, and then the moon rose and she saw the ship, outline against the sky, riding at anchor in the bay.

She had never been on a boat before and a faint excitement stirred in her.

The gangplank was steep and the guide-ropes rough beneath her palms. A man with his hair greased into a stiff pigtail lifted her to a narrow deck and then they were all crowding below into a cabin with hammocks slung from the low beams. They were casting off. Anne could hear the slap of rope on the deck and shouted orders. The Earl, bent double in the inadequate space, ducked out on to the deck with George of Clarence behind him.

Isobel's voice rose fretfully. 'Why cannot George stay with me? I feel sick!'

'We have not even cast off properly, so you cannot possibly feel sick,' the Countess said firmly. 'Anne, this place is positively airless. Go up on deck and find out if there is another cabin. We cannot possibly be all crammed in here for the entire voyage.'

Anne trailed up the short ladder that led to the deck and stood in the deep shadow watching the pigtailed figures swarming over the rigging.

Her sleepiness had vanished and she drew a deep breath of the salt wind. It was, after all, something of an adventure to be leaving England for the first time in her life. There was no profit in remembering how Richard's hands had gripped her own as he promised that he would wait, and there was certainly no profit in remembering the sewing maid and her babe. For all Anne knew her own father had sired many bastards, though she doubted whether her mother would have allowed it. A small chuckle escaped her and the Earl came over from the rail where he had been leaning.

'Not abed yet, daughter? We'll be in the open channel soon and then the vessel may begin to pitch and toss,' he said kindly.

'I wondered if there was another cabin,' she said. 'My lady mother says we will be sadly cramped.'

'There's no help for it, sweetheart. The one cabin will have to suffice,' he said ruefully. 'I shall sleep on deck with George.'

'Not the most comfortable accommodation for a prince of the blood royal,' George remarked gloomily. 'I begin to think we should have marched on London.'

'A brave show we'd have made,' the Earl said sarcastically. 'By the Rood, milord Clarence, but you chatter a deal of nonsense!'

'In which I am not alone!' the Duke snapped. 'I seem to recall your saying the entire country would whirl me to the throne in a matter of weeks! So far we have had signally little success in our campaign!'

'Perhaps if you had behaved more like a leader more men would have flocked to our standard!'

'Every time I try to give an order you countermand it,' George said sulkily.

Their altercation was interrupted by a sudden scream from the cabin below. Anne's hair prickled at the back of her neck, but her mother's voice followed reassuringly.

'Isobel has the cramp! It is no more than that, but she needs room to breathe. Can you find another cabin?'

'There are none,' the Earl informed her, going to the ladder and peering down.

'Then bed Anne up on deck with you, and find an oil-lamp! We cannot manage without light!'

'It is the child!' the Duke said in agitation. 'I knew the jolting would be too much for her.'

As if to underline his words, there issued another sobbing cry from the cabin.

'Anne, go down and help your mother,' the Earl said. 'George, there is absolutely nothing for you to get excited about! The poor girl probably has a false labour, that's all. Very common at seven months. Anne, are you going?'

'Yes, Father.'

She went obediently, her eyes adjusting to the gloom in which Isobel lay, moaning and tossing, while the Countess piled cushions about her.

'It may be the babe come early,' she said in a low voice, drawing Anne aside. 'If we're fortunate the pains will die down and we'll be able to land before she gives birth, but the jolting of the horse was too much for her, I fear.'

'What do you wish me to do?' Anne asked.

'Nothing for the moment. Go up on deck and sleep until morning. I'll call you if I need you.'

Her mother patted her briskly and turned back to Isobel, who was tossing and turning again, her face contorted with pain. If that was what happened when one had a baby, then Anne hoped that she herself would not have a large family. The Earl had made a bed up for her out of rugs and a spare pallet, and she curled up thankfully, finding the rocking of the boat as it headed into the open sea a soothing sensation.

It was the last peaceful night she was to know during the voyage. By morning Isobel's pains had increased in frequency and intensity and Anne was needed to help the Countess in the stuffy cabin. There was pathetically little they could do, save stop the writhing girl from flinging herself out of the hammock and keep watch during her intervals of restless slumber.

There was a bitter disappointment awaiting them at Calais. The Governor sent out a boat before they could drop anchor, forbidding them to land but conveying wine for the ladies' comfort.

'Wenlock has spoken up for Edward and will not help us,' the Earl said. 'We will sail westward to Honfleur. I am certain that Louis will receive us with honour.'

He had come down into the cabin to acquaint his wife with the news and she turned a haggard face towards him, crying bitterly,

'Honour is useless when we need a refuge, my lord! Isobel is in sad case and will be in worse if we do not get medical attention for her soon!'

'There is nothing I can do. You must shift for yourself,' he answered with unwonted sharpness.

'As if women ever did anything else!' the Countess muttered. 'Isobel, you must bear down hard when the pain comes, and take quick, short breaths between.'

'I am going to die!' poor Isobel moaned, her pretty face blotched and swollen, her fair hair dank with sweat.

'You are going to be all right, child,' her mother said firmly. 'Anne, come and hold your sister's other hand. Isobel, bear down! Dear God, but I shall be glad when we reach Honfleur!'

An hour before they sighted the French port Isobel's child was born. A waxen-faced boy who never drew breath he lay, wrapped in white linen, a look of infinite contempt on his face for a world he had never known. George of Clarence was kneeling by his weakly wailing Isobel, and the Countess looked every day of her 44 years as she stared into the face of her dead grandchild.

'He must be buried at sea,' Isobel insisted, choking back her tears. 'Poor little wight! He is so perfect in every detail.'

'We will have other babes,' her husband consoled. 'When I am made King — .'

'I don't wish you to be King,' she said fretfully. 'Kings are always running away or marching to battle! I want us to live peacefully as Duke and Duchess!'

Anne felt sick and shaken after the long hours of her sister's labour. It had been heartrending to witness Isobel's distress and the foetid stench of the cabin turned her stomach. She went up on deck, glad of the sharp breeze that stung her cheeks and left salt on her lips. Her father stood by the rail, conferring with the ship's captain, and she went to him, stumbling a little from tiredness.

'We'll be landing soon, chuck.' He put his arm about her. 'You can glimpse the shore line afar off. We'll be kindly received.'

'And Isobel's babe?' She looked up at him enquiringly.

'We'll consign the poor babe to the water. It was come too soon, hinny.'

'Isobel doesn't want George to be made King,' she confided, leaning against him.

'As to that we shall see,' the Earl said, and his tone was abstracted as if he had forgotten all about her.

6

It was winter. Snow lay thickly over the rooftops and hung frozen from the eaves, and in the moat the pages had tied bones to their shoes and were sliding up and down, holding on to one another. Their laughter drifted up to the window above where Anne stood, gazing down at the animated scene.

She was richly and beautifully clad in a dress of deep pink silk patterned with bronze and gold over an undertunic of bronze velvet. The high neck of the gown and the tight cuffs of the full sleeves were banded in dark fur. Her long hair was brushed loosely over her shoulders under a veil of gold tissue. Her eyelids had been painted gold and carmine brightened her wide mouth. She stood so still, her hands at her sides, that a casual passer-by, glancing up at the narrow embrasure, might have been forgiven for imagining that a brightly painted statue had been placed there.

Behind the elaborately gowned little figure the long, high-ceilinged chamber stretched, warmed by two enormous fires that blazed in the twin hearths at each side of the table where the royal family were eating a private dinner. If she turned her head she would see them. King Louis with his odd, unmatching garments, for his vanity lay in having no vanity, the Countess in a gown of purple sewn with gold stars, the Duchess Isobel lovelier than ever in a blue dress. At the other side of the table, their backs to her, were the two people she hated and feared more than anyone else in the world. Margaret of Anjou and her son, Edward, sat with loosely clasped hands as if to emphasise their affection. They were even dressed alike in the vivid crimson, gold and turquoise of their ducal banners. Anne's own fingers clenched slightly. They were brilliant with rings, the rubies, emeralds and diamonds flashing fire as the thin, December sunshine beamed upon them. Few girls of 14 had such jewels, but she thought, with a sad resignation beyond her years, that she was now truly poor.

They had begun so well, being greeted at Honfleur with a salute of cannon, flags hastily strung across the narrow streets, and messages of welcome from King Louis. The Earl had galloped off to Amboise, leaving his family comfortably lodged in an hotel to cheer Isobel, who was slowly recovering from the pain and sorrow of her premature labour.

Then late in July the Earl had returned, a great train of French noblemen following him, to announce that he had come to a most satisfactory agreement with King Louis.

'He has arranged to back us with troops and weapons in time for us to invade England before the autumn gales begin,' he said with satisfaction beaming in his smile. 'I have decided that no good end is to be served by putting George on the throne. He has no real support, I fear.'

George, holding Isobel's hand, flushed deeply but said nothing.

'His Grace of France, in return for an alliance against Burgundy, is prepared to restore King Henry to the throne,' the Earl continued. 'Queen Margaret and I are now reconciled.'

There was a stunned silence. Then the Countess, apparently collecting her scattered wits exclaimed, 'So you will put Lancaster upon the throne again. What of poor Isobel, who hoped to be Queen?'

'I have a more useful match in mind,' her husband said. 'It has taken much diplomatic skill to arrange, for Queen Margaret still distrusts my intentions, but we have betrothed her son, Ned, to our own little Anne.'

Even now, five months later, Anne could still feel the cold, sick horror that had gripped her. In her peaked face her eyes had grown enormous, her cheekbones standing out sharply.

'The Queen agreed to the betrothal only, and the marriage will not be solemnised until England is taken again.'

So there was the chance of a reprieve. Edward of England might still beat back the Earl from his shores. Then she would not be married to this prince she had never seen. Guilt flooded her as she realised that, in essence, she was hoping for her father to be defeated, and her shoulders drooped as she realised also that even the Earl's defeat would not secure her marriage to Richard.

'And what of me?' The Duke of Clarence had found his voice. 'What of me, milord of Warwick? You won me to you by fair promises!'

'Which I hoped to fulfil,' the Earl said sadly, 'but it was not the will of the people, my dear boy. One promise I will certainly keep to you. If Anne and Ned of Lancaster have no issue, then you or your children shall reign.'

'Has Queen Margaret agreed to

that?' the Countess asked.

'Reluctantly.' The Earl smiled grimly, recalling Margaret of Anjou's cold and haughty demeanour as she had agreed to the terms. 'But she knows I am her last hope if she wishes to set her witless husband on the throne again.'

'When will you sail?' the Countess asked.

'Within the month,' he said. 'George, you will come with me, of course. We will send word when we land and word of our victory.'

'So! Henry of Lancaster will rule again,' the Countess said slowly.

'We must move with the temper of the times,' her husband said. 'Henry will rule again, and Edward Plantagenet will learn that a Neville cannot be treated with ingratitude.'

It was not poor King Henry who would rule, Anne thought. It was her father. Her father had always known what was best for the country, and it was disloyal to think that he would not do his best for both his daughters. And the victory was not yet in his grasp. Perhaps when he and George reached England they would decide to support Edward again.

They had left, as the Earl had said, before the month had run its course. Anne had stood with Isobel on the balcony of the hotel, watching the mercenaries whom Louis had paid marching past with pikes fixed and banners fluttering. She had stood very still, schooling her face to quietness, hearing Isobel's suppressed sobs as if they came from a long way off.

It was impossible for her to wish them well with a truthful heart, but she dreaded hearing of their deaths or capture.

Word came on the October tide, and the Countess, her usual poise swept away by excitement, hurried into the chamber where her daughters sat, a document in her hand.

'It is all completed!' she exclaimed. 'It is a splendid victory, my loves. A complete reversal of our fortunes! Your father did not even have to fight. Your uncle John was the instrument of it.'

'How?' It was Isobel who asked, for Anne's throat had closed up and she stared mutely.

'John served Edward well and was ill-rewarded when Edward stripped him of his earldom of Northumberland and gave it back to Harry Percy. So, when your father landed, John spoke for King Henry and vowed his forces to Lancaster. Your father and George entered London in triumph without having to strike a blow. King Henry was brought from the Tower and cheered through the streets, and the Woodville queen is fled into Westminster Sanctuary with her three girls! That proud bitch has insulted the Nevilles for the last time!'

'What of Edward?' Isobel asked.

'Fled! He and Richard and Lord Hastings and the Queen's brother, Anthony, all fled to Burgundy! They will settle down in exile, I've no doubt.'

'When do we go to England?' Isobel asked eagerly.

'Your father intends to establish a strong government,' the Countess said, 'but in spring we will all go back to England. All of us! First we must communicate with Queen Margaret and remind her of her pledge.'

The pledge that if the Earl put back her witless husband on the throne she would marry her son to the Earl's daughter. Something long suppressed rose up in Anne and she heard her voice, thin and high, crying,

'But my lord father promised that I was to be married to Richard of Gloucester!'

'Richard is of no political importance,' her mother said. 'As the bride of Edward of Lancaster you stand in direct line to the throne after King Henry dies.'

'Richard was our friend,' Anne said whitely.

'My dear, I have nothing against the lad!' the Countess said irritably. 'I am sorry if you are disappointed, my love, but we must learn to face realities! We cannot spend our days in dreaming. Prince Edward is 16 and a lusty youngling from all accounts, so you have no real cause for complaint!'

Anne was effectively silenced. The habit of engrained obedience was too strong. Only peasants married where they pleased.

'So Anne will be Queen one day,' Isobel said. Her tone was discontented, and the Countess frowned at her.

'You must not begrudge your sister her good fortune,' she said sharply. 'She must wed a lad she has never seen, and you are married to a young man for whom you feel love-liking.'

So she was not entirely unaware of Anne's bitter disappointment. It would make no difference. Anne was to be married off as part of the new treaty, and the Countess would not lift a finger to alter matters.

Within another month they had travelled to Amboise, where a graceful, pinnacled château rose above its moat. It was snowing as the ladies were borne along in their leather-sided litters, and the few cottages they passed along the way were no more than hovels, the peasants gaunt faced and hollow-cheeked. Anne, wrapped in furs, wondered if it was snowing in Burgundy too, and if Richard, in his exile, knew that she was to be wed to Margaret of Anjou's son. He would surely understand that she was not entering into the marriage of her own free will. Wistfully she tried to hope that somehow or other he would rescue her. How it might be contrived she had no idea, but it made the journey bearable to think that such an event might be possible.

She had dreaded her first meeting with the French Queen and her son, and it had been as bad as she had feared.

The beautiful princess of 15 who had been brought from France to marry the gentle, unworldly Henry VI was now a handsome, hard-eyed woman of 40, her hair already streaked with grey, her paint failing to disguise the network of lines at the corners of her eyes and mouth. At her side a tall, fair-haired boy held himself erect.

Anne's heart sank as she saw the sulkiness on his rather full mouth, and heard the icy note in his mother's voice as she said,

'So this is Lady Anne? She does not look 14 yet.'

'She was always very small for her age, Your Grace,' the Countess said.

Anne longed to cry out, 'Don't apologise for me! This woman would not be preparing to remount her throne if my lord father had not agreed to help her to it!' Instead she sank into a deep curtsy, masking her rage and embarrassment under a small, courtly smile.

'Well, the marriage is agreed, and the girl looks healthy,' Margaret of Anjou said. 'I see no reason to delay the ceremony. The Vicar of Bayeux has agreed to officiate. We have obtained a dispensation from the Patriarch of Jerusalem.'

'Surely the Holy Father — ,' the Countess ventured.

'The Patriarch of Jerusalem is perfectly capable of issuing a dispensation,' Queen Margaret said coldly.

'Of course, Your Grace. I am naturally concerned that the marriage should be legal,' the Countess said smoothly.

'And so that Your Grace does not seek to wriggle out of the arrangements later,' her eyes added.

'I would never permit my dear son to be illegally mated,' the Queen said.

'Even if your daughter is plain and undersized,' her smile added.

Anne, still on one knee, shifted her weight to the other foot and prayed silently for a wind to sweep her up and carry her off to Burgundy. No wind came, but the prince took her hand and raised her, and said, his voice edged with mockery,

'Why, my Lady Anne, we will have to mount you on stilts!'

'Or chop off your legs, Your Grace,'

she bit back, her eyes narrowing.

'Your daughter has a sharp tongue, my Lady of Warwick,' the Queen said. 'She must take care lest she cut herself.'

'Anne has always been a most dutiful daughter,' the Countess said quickly.

'One hopes she will also be a most dutiful wife,' Queen Margaret said, contriving to look as if she, for one, had the gravest doubts.

'The Neville women always follow their lords,' the Countess said.

'Which must make you somewhat dizzy,' Queen Margaret said sweetly, 'as my lord Warwick changes direction so often!'

'The winds of change,' the Countess murmured.

'Blew you to France and your girl into my son's bed. Let us all go into the chapel to pray that the union is a fruitful one. Anne, you may walk with me, girl. If you are to be the future Queen of England you must learn to comport yourself with dignity.'

Anne threw an imploring glance

towards her mother, but the Countess was suddenly very busy rearranging the folds of her skirt.

Now, standing at the window and looking into the ice-bound moat, Anne had never felt more miserable in her life. The marriage had taken place an hour before in the chapel of Amboise and it had been a quiet affair, as if Queen Margaret sought to deny any glory to a Neville bride. A handful of noblemen and their ladies had witnessed the ceremony and the Nuptial Mass that followed. She had made her responses in a flat little voice and not once allowed herself to think of Richard or of Middleham, both of which seemed to belong to some other girl's life.

The ceremony over, King Louis had kissed her and given her a bag of gold, and she had flung the coins from a balcony into a space beyond the gates where a crowd of ragged people scrambled for them eagerly. One girl, her hands chapped and raw had gazed

146

up enviously at the bride, and Anne had wanted to shout down to her, 'Don't envy me! I am a poor maid for all my finery.'

'If you stand at that window you will take cold, child,' the King said, coming to her side.

'I am quite strong, Sire,' Anne said, but she moved obediently nearer to the fire.

'This ought to be a happy day for you,' Louis said, giving her a faintly concerned glance. 'Wed to the son of a King of England; your father returned to his allegiance; yourself not yet 15 with all your life ahead of you! This ought to be a very happy day.'

'I know, Sire.'

'Your bridegroom is a fine lad, devoted to his mother,' the King went on.

'And his father, King Henry?' She raised troubled eyes to his ugly face and said, 'I have always been told he is — wanting in his wits, poor soul.'

'Poor soul indeed!' he echoed,

'Henry is an innocent, my dear. From time to time one crops up in our family. My grandfather now, who was Henry's grandfather too, believed he was made of glass, and my own father was mocked for his awkwardness. Saved by Jeanne de Arc who treated him with very great respect. You English burned her and Henry watched the burning. He was only six years old then, and there are those who say that he turned away from the real world after that and devoted himself to prayer and the angelic world. You have no cause to fear King Henry. It is his queen with whom you must treat.'

Lowering her voice Anne said nervously, 'She does not like me, Your Grace.'

'She would like you very well if she had not been constrained to marry you to her son,' he told her. 'She is my niece and I know her nature well. She is a brave woman and a greatly wronged one and you must try to understand her side of the case.'

'Nobody tries to understand my side of it,' Anne thought with a flash of resentment. Aloud she said meekly,

'I shall try to be a good daughter to her.'

The intimate dinner-party was winding to its close. Queen Margaret was rising, leading her son to where the French King stood with Anne.

'She is a trifle overcome by the solemnity of the occasion,' Louis said. 'She is very young, Margaret.'

'A year younger than I was when I travelled to England to be wed to King Henry.'

'Ah, but you had certain natural advantages, Your Grace. You were both spirited and beautiful,' he returned.

'And condemned to be with a husband who was more monk than man! Anne will have a lustier bridegroom than the one with whom I bedded!'

'Speaking of which — .' King Louis paused delicately.

'Aye, it is time they were left alone in

order to become acquainted.' Queen Margaret turned and made some gesture to the other ladies, who rose as promptly as if she had jerked strings.

Silently Anne watched them file out, her mother lingering to bestow a smile, the French King taking his niece's arm. A servant closed the double doors and the laughter from the moat below grew fainter.

'They are not formally bedding us,' Prince Edward said.

'It is too early to go to bed,' Anne nodded and, to her chagrin, heard herself tittering nervously. To hide it she went over to the table and began to eat a pear, peeling the skin down with her sharp nails.

'What a great baby you must be!' he exclaimed. 'Hasn't your lady mother ever told you about the duties of a wife?'

'Yes, of course.' She remembered having been interested and slightly shocked to picture her dignified parents engaged in such antics.

'Then we must do likewise.' He came and stood opposite to her.

'It is not time for bed,' she repeated desperately.

'We must do our duty,' he said stiffly. 'Marriage is a great responsibility, my mother says, and we must face up to responsibilities. The crown must be provided with heirs — '

'I wish you would stop quoting your mother at me!'

In a spasm of nervous irritation she flung the core of the pear into the middle of the table.

'My mother is a great warrior queen and my father is a saint,' he said.

'Your mother needs *my* father's help before she can get back her throne!' Anne retorted.

'And because she needs that help I have to be wed to a silly baby,' he said contemptuously.

'And I never had the smallest desire to be wed to you!' Anne said with spirit.

'You look prettier when you're angry,' he said consideringly. 'When I first saw you I thought you the plainest thing I ever saw in my life, even though you are not pock-marked. Now you begin to look almost comely.'

'I am not in the least interested in your opinion of me,' Anne said, haughtily swishing her skirt aside.

An instant later she was caught and held tightly and Prince Edward was kissing her. For a moment she was so surprised that she hung limply within his arms and then, scarlet with rage and disgust, she began to struggle furiously, twisting her head aside and kicking at his shins in a vain attempt to be free.

The silk of her overdress ripped and she hit out blindly, her rings splitting the boy's lip. As blood spurted he momentarily relaxed his grip, and she whirled away, snatching up a goblet and holding it over her head.

'You come near me and I'll kill you! I swear I'll kill you, Ned Plantagenet! Don't you touch me! Don't touch me!'

All her disappointment and all her confusion spilled out in a scarlet rage.

The Prince seemed to her to stand in a haze of crimson and to grow taller even as she stood there.

The door opened and a tall figure rustled in, stood for a moment surveying the scene, and then walked forward, brows raised and voice coolly amused.

'Getting to know each other?' Queen Margaret asked.

'Madam, he attacked me!' Anne exclaimed, lowering her arm but still holding onto the goblet.

'She's my wife and supposed to submit to me!' Prince Edward cried.

'I won't be submissive where there is no love-liking!' Anne said violently.

She was shaking from head to foot, but her face was set in mutinous lines.

'Put down the cup, my dear,' the Queen said, her voice still amused, though her eyes had narrowed slightly.

Anne put the goblet down and stood in humiliating embarrassment, while the Queen swept past to stand between them.

'Ned, a husband should gently persuade his wife,' she chided. 'I said you were a lusty lad but that does not give you licence to tear the Lady Anne's dress. What happened to your lip?'

'It was an accident,' Ned said.

'I hit him,' Anne said. 'I meant to hit him.'

'So you have spirit. A pity you could not employ it to better ends than to fight with your wedded husband,' the Queen said dryly.

'Madam, I know he is my husband now,' Anne said shiveringly, 'but must we be bedded yet? Cannot we wait for a few months? Until I am older?'

'You are past 14. Many younger brides have borne children,' the Prince argued.

The thought of bearing a child to this rough, sulky lad was a horrible one. Anne felt the tears start into her eyes and her legs were trembling so much that she wished it was etiquette to sit down without permission.

Margaret of Anjou was chewing her lip thoughtfully, plans behind her eyes. If this wretched marriage were not consummated she would have a trump card to throw into the balance against the Earl of Warwick. An unconsummated marriage could be annulled and Edward married to a more suitable bride.

Anne was crying openly now, tears splashing on to her torn bodice and dripping on to her fingers. Ned was dabbing at his cut lip and glowering in a manner that threatened one of his frequent storms of temper.

'Perhaps we were too precipitate,' Queen Margaret said slowly. 'It is much better for so young a bride to be given some space of time in which to grow accustomed to being a wife. A year's delay would harm nobody.'

'Oh, Your Grace, that would be so kind of you!' Anne breathed.

'A resting space between altar and bed to enable both of you to become more friendly, and for my Lady Anne to grow a little,' Margaret purred. 'You are so narrow of hip, my dear, that I fear the consequences of a too early confinement.'

'It suits me well enough,' Ned said rudely. 'I didn't want to sleep with her anyway!'

'Ah, you will alter your mind as you grow to know her better,' his mother said, passing Anne a napkin with which to dry her streaming eyes. 'Tomorrow we will travel to Paris and wait there until we receive word to return to England. You will like Paris, Anne. It is a most beautiful city and my apartments there are full of fine treasures.'

'Why cannot we return to England now?' her son demanded. 'Why cannot I be permitted to fight for my father's throne?'

'Because Edward of York is fled and there is nobody to fight,' the Queen said patiently. 'When spring comes and the entire country is subdued, then we will all return in triumph. There will be processions through the streets and Te Deums sung.'

'And we will see my lord father again!'

'Aye, that too.' The Queen spoke with a certain dryness. The last time she had seen her wedded lord he had cried out that she was Medusa and had come to turn him into stone.

'I am most grateful for Your Grace's understanding,' Anne said, red-eyed.

'My dear child, I hope I am woman enough to sympathise with a little maidenly shrinking,' Margaret said. 'It is becoming in a maid to be shy, and we lose nothing by a little delay.'

'I think it's an excellent notion,' the Prince said defiantly. 'If we are not bedded, I will be able to choose a wife who pleases me better.'

'Must you keep on bleeding?' the Queen interrupted frowningly, uneasily conscious that her son was echoing her own thought. 'Come, we'll put some ice on it.'

She swept her son ahead of her,

pausing to smile over her shoulder at Anne. The poor girl looked quite ugly with the tip of her nose red and the paint standing out sharply on her thin cheeks.

The double doors closed behind them, and Anne sat down abruptly, putting her face into her hands, letting the shaking overcome her completely. She felt a surge of mixed emotions. Relief at the unexpected reprieve and gratitude for the Queen's understanding mingled with anger and a feeling of intense shame. The Prince's kiss had violated her in the deepest part of herself, for during one split second, when his mouth had pressed upon hers, she had experienced an answering leap of some feeling unknown.

It was disloyal of her even to admit to such a feeling, and she shuddered violently, muttering fiercely to herself, 'Loyalty binds me.'

It was her talisman against the future that stretched bleakly ahead. In her mind she saw it as a long road leading to darkness, and behind her was a sunlit childhood but she could not, at this moment, remember it very clearly.

7

They were going home. The phrase had a magnetic ring, so magical that Anne had been repeating it at intervals throughout the voyage. Such a different journey it had been from the one the previous year when Isobel's babe had been stillborn. Whatever lay ahead they were returning to England.

The Countess and Isobel had landed at Portsmouth. Anne was with Queen Margaret and Prince Edward on the larger and more elaborate vessel. She liked the Prince no better than when she had been wed to him four months before, but she was beginning to feel more at ease with the formidable Queen Margaret, who was, if not exactly motherly, never actively unkind.

There had been nothing but rumours from England for weeks past, most of them conflicting. Edward and Richard had sailed from Burgundy with a force of 1,000 men, but a storm had scattered his few ships. Edward and Richard had landed at separate ports and lost their way. So many rumours and none of them able to be checked.

'We land at Weymouth and wait for milords Somerset and Exeter to escort us to London,' Queen Margaret said. 'I am hoping for news of the capture of the rebel dukes.'

The rebel dukes being Edward, Anne supposed. Everything had turned upside down again.

Now they were waiting to disembark, and despite her anxiety she felt a thrill of excitement. The sun was shining and a crowd of people waited on the quay, many of them already kneeling. The Queen, her son at her side, made her way with slow dignity down the gangplank to where horses and a litter were waiting. A man in the livery of Lancaster stepped forward and bowed respectfully.

'God give you welcome, Your Grace. I am bidden to escort your party to Cerne Abbey to wait word from the Earl of Warwick.'

'Where is the Earl? What news?' the Queen asked sharply, gesturing to the man to rise.

'We don't know, Your Grace. There are some say the Duke of York and his brother of Gloucester are at Tewkesbury, but nothing is definite,' the man said. 'His Grace, King Henry is in London, which is being held in His Grace's name, and there is a great force led by Warwick's brother against the Duke Edward.'

'I spiked his father's and brother's heads over the gate of York,' Margaret said with sudden fierceness, 'and I'll have the heads of Edward and Gloucester on London Bridge before the month is out.'

'Duke Edward's wife has borne a son in the Sanctuary of Westminster,' the man volunteered.

'Well, there's a child who will never

see his father!' the Queen said. 'Mount up, Edward. Anne, you may take the litter. For myself I prefer to be in the saddle.'

She was already spurring ahead, and Anne climbed up into the litter, pulling her veil down over her face. As they jolted towards the abbey she could hear the thin cheering of the crowd pressing about the Queen's horse.

There was a meal waiting for them in a chamber behind the refectory and a further chamber had been fitted with beds for the ladies. Anne could eat little. Her ears were constantly pricked for the galloping of hooves, the sound of voices raised above the low chanting of the monks. The Queen, too, was in distracted mood, constantly rising to pace the floor, her fingers tapping the sill as she gazed through the slit windows into the cloisters beyond.

It was near dusk when the clattering of harness and the clip-clop of shod mounts came at last. The Queen whirled about, her face lighting up.

'My lord of Somerset, what cheer have you for me?' she demanded of the travel-stained nobleman who hurried in.

'No cheer, Your Grace.' He dropped hastily to his knee, his words spilling out in a torrent. 'Edward of York marched unopposed to Barnet, ten miles north of London. John Neville held back his troops until the Duke had passed, and at Barnet milord Clarence joined them.'

'Joined whom? What are you babbling?' Queen Margaret cried.

'Joined his brothers, Your Grace. They were reconciled on the field, all three swearing love and fidelity.'

'And the Earl? What happened to Warwick? Milord Oxford?' The Queen shook Somerset's arm violently.

'Killed,' Somerset said heavily. 'The Earl of Warwick was slain on the field, and milord Oxford is fled. Oh, and Warwick's brother is killed too. He brought his men out against the Duke at the last, but some say his own men killed him, fearing he would change sides again.'

Anne had risen from her seat at the table and stood now, pressed against the wall so hard that she could imagine herself melting into the stone.

'The bodies of Warwick and his brother, John, were stripped and laid out on the pavement of St Paul's Cathedral for all to see,' Somerset was telling them.

'Then all is lost.' The Queen spoke in the accents of despair.

'No, Your Grace. The King is still King, and the gentry of Devon and Cornwall have risen for Lancaster. I am here to bid Your Grace ride with all speed into Wales.'

'Wales? In God's name, why Wales?' she demanded. 'Why not London?'

'Sir Jasper Tudor is calling out the chieftains in support of His Grace King Henry,' Somerset panted out, gulping wine from the goblet she thrust at him. 'If Your Grace and Prince Edward make all speed to cross the Severn at Gloucester we can sweep back with Welsh reinforcements and take the three dukes.'

'My father is slain?' Anne's small, shaking voice rose into the silence. 'Uncle John too? It isn't true, is it? It cannot be true!'

'And your *precious* brother-in-law crawled back into the bosom of his *precious* family!' the Queen snapped.

'My father dead,' Anne repeated, but the words still made no sense. Her father was the Kingmaker and without his powerful presence the world was a grey place. 'It will kill my lady mother! It will kill her!'

'Her Grace of Warwick has gone into Sanctuary at Beaulieu Abbey,' Somerset told her, catching his breath and looking at her with sympathy. 'Duchess Isobel is on her way to join the Duke of Clarence.'

'I want to go to my mother,' Anne said. 'Please, I want to go home to my lady mother.'

'Your place is with your husband,' the Queen said.

'But he's not — we have never — I want to go to my lady mother. I am of no use now,' Anne stammered, tears thickening her voice. 'Please, Your Grace, I want my mother!'

'Control yourself, girl!' Queen Margaret's voice whipped her. 'Pray try not to make a nuisance of yourself. I have neither the time nor the inclination to waste it upon you now! Milord Somerset, have you horses ready and escort for a night march?'

'Your grace, thousands are streaming to your banner,' he assured her. 'The Governor of Calais has brought his liegemen and Courtenay of Devon has mustered his yeomen.'

'Then we'll to horse.' The Queen snapped her fingers, her eyes glittering. 'If we move fast we can outwit Edward before he has gathered full support. Come!'

She was all fire and energy. Anne, tears dried at their source by her growing sense of horror, stumbled after them.

She had never ridden with an army before and her spirit shrank from the torchlit faces under the steel caps, the starlight glittering on the fixed pikes and burnished shields, the banners waving on the tall poles, the rattling of the wheels on the supply wagons, the neighing of the horses as they plodded through the dust-laden lanes.

Pain and weariness had numbed her and she jogged on in silence, a heavy cloak shrouding her thin shoulders, her face enveloped in its concealing hood.

They reached Bristol and she was helped down from her saddle and supported through an arched gateway and up a curving flight of steps to a chamber where a warm bed waited her.

The days, she was never certain how many, passed in a stupor of grief. She could no longer make sense of the world. Her father, who had put Edward upon the throne, was now dead and with him the uncle who had warned her to keep her nose out of treasons and been of divided loyalties himself. Richard, who had vowed to wait for her, was now chasing after her in enmity and George had changed sides again. She envied Isobel, on her way to meet the man she loved and had been allowed to marry, and she wept tearlessly for her mother who, in Sanctuary at Beaulieu, would be in great agony of mind.

Nobody took any notice of her. The Queen seemed tirelessly consulting with the captains and lieutenants who rode in and out of the gates of the city. The Prince was wild with excitement at the prospect of his first taste of battle and spent hours strutting up and down in his armour. Queen Margaret herself wore a steel corselet over her bodice and declared herself ready to give battle.

'The Welsh chieftains are raising their standard at Hereford. We will make a night march to Gloucester and cross the river there,' she said energetically.

So it was the hour to ride again. Anne had hoped that she might be left behind in Bristol but feared to suggest it lest her mother-in-law's uncertain temper be directed against her. They ate a hasty supper and streamed through the gates, the knights bunched closely behind the leaders, the foot-soldiers alternately jogging and marching. There had seemed thousands of them within the confines of the city, but strung along the road, they were a long, straggling line that tailed into nothingness.

It was eerie to be riding in darkness, only the flaring torches bordering the way. Once or twice Anne fell asleep and woke with a jerk to hear the steady slap of leather against flesh as a detachment of archers loped past at the trot, their full quivers banging against their thighs.

Dawn was a symphony of pink and gold, the sun coming up behind the eastern ridges to illumine the walls of Gloucester wrapped still in the mist of early morning. For an instant Anne's heart lifted. The word had a blessed and familiar ring. One day she would be Duchess of Gloucester. She was not certain how such an event was to come about, but at scarce 15 one has the right to believe in miracles.

'Your Grace!' One of the scouts galloped up, sweat streaked. 'Your Grace, the gates of the city are closed and the soldiers on the walls shout for Edward of York!'

'Can we attack?' the Queen asked Somerset.

'With reports of the Duke's forces coming up behind? It would be suicide, madam,' he answered curtly.

'We can cross the river at Tewkesbury?'

'And gather reinforcements in Wales? Aye, Your Grace, but the men are weary after a night's march,' he began.

'We are all weary,' she said impatiently. 'The Lady Anne sleeps as she rides, but she has not complained once. We go on to Tewkesbury!'

The sun rose higher and hotter,

browning the hedgerows. Sweat ran down the men's faces from under the brims of their leather hats, and the banners drooped forlornly in the still air. Anne's own face was pale and damp, and her breath came in little gasps. Once they paused briefly to relieve themselves behind a stone wall, and a soldier brought them some water in his hat.

Mounting up again Anne caught the Queen's eyes fixed upon her. There was approval in them and the dawning of affection.

'You have courage, girl,' she said. 'As much as any in the realm, I'd wager, for all your lack of inches!'

'I thank your Grace.' Anne managed to summon a wan smile as they moved off again.

'Why cannot we turn and fight?' the Prince demanded.

'Because we must join up with Sir Jasper Tudor,' his mother said impatiently. 'Never fear, Ned! We'll give no quarter when we take our stand!'

The Tudors were half-kin to King Henry. Anne had never met any of them but had heard they were red-haired and clever. Edmund had wed the Beautfort heiress and died before the birth of his son, Harry, now being reared in Brittany. Jasper was Harry Tudor's uncle and reputed to be devoted to his nephew. Loyalty binds me, Anne thought. But there were so many different loyalties and her own were in confusion.

There were fewer men in the long train that followed them, snaking northward through the dry and dusty lanes. Many had stumbled away from the main lines to lie exhausted on the grass, and the occasional bursts of singing that had cheered the earlier part of the journey had died away into silence.

'Your Grace, we will have to make camp!' Somerset spoke with desperation in his voice. 'The men cannot go on! We have the Yorkists on our tails as it is.'

'If we make camp tonight can word be sent to the Welsh to join us here?' the Queen demanded.

'I can send a couple of scouts across the river to contact Sir Jasper,' Wenlock put in.

'Then we'll make camp on the high ground. Are there chaplains to hear confession?'

'Aye, madam, but the men need sleep, not prayers.'

'They may have both,' she said. 'Can we obtain supplies from Tewkesbury?'

'I'll give orders, Your Grace, for meat and bread.'

'The Prince and I will go into Tewkesbury,' the Queen began.

'No.' The Prince expostulated. 'I won't be hidden away with the females while men die in my cause! You promised me a taste of battle!'

'My son, you are not yet 17,' she said.

'I am old enough to fight,' he argued. 'My father is in London and so it is my task to act as rallying point for the troops.'

'I could ride myself. Women have done so before,' the Queen said.

'Before God, my lady mother, would you shame me before the whole army?' he asked, his face flushing darkly. 'How will it fadge if the soldiers see me sheltered by the skirts of my mother? The heir of Lancaster must fight!'

'The Prince is right, madam,' Somerset said. 'You and the Lady Anne must retire to a place of safety and Prince Edward will remain with the army.'

'That building over there down the stream,' the Queen pointed. 'What is it?'

'A convent, Your Grace. I believe it is a Poor Clare foundation.'

'Anne and I will seek shelter there. Ned, you will be sensible? Do not expose yourself to any unnecessary danger. You are England's heir, the hope of Lancaster. My lord of Somerset, if my boy is hurt I swear I'll have your head!' The Queen spoke rapidly, the colour ebbing and flowing in her face.

'Madam, you have my word on it,' Somerset said, clenched hand to his heart.

They rode with a small escort down the narrow track to the small greystone building set so close to the narrow river that the splashing of water drowned the birdsong around. Away to the right the walls of Tewkesbury were dwarfed by the high towers of the abbey, and the rough ground was swarming with weary men dragging themselves into battle formation, for in preparation for a dawn onslaught, they would sleep where they intended to fight.

The Prioress, who was a gentle soul with unexpectedly shrewed blue eyes, bowed gravely to the royal ladies. She spoke to the Queen, assuring her that the resources of the convent would be at her disposal.

'Including our prayers, of course. Our accommodation is limited but we can make you comfortable.'

The room to which they were shown had a curious stark charm, but Anne was too tired to appreciate anything but the pallet to which she was directed.

She was woken at dawn by the soft chanting of the nuns in choir and the pacing of the Queen as she walked restlessly from one end of the chamber to the other.

'Your Grace?' Anne sat up hastily, pushing back the long hair that tumbled about her shoulders. 'Is there news?'

'The fighting has begun,' Queen Margaret said, 'and would God that I were there!'

'Madam, women do not ride into battle,' Anne said.

'No, it is their task to wait,' the Queen said. 'That is the hardest part of all.'

'Is the — is the army of the Yorkists very large?'

'They are attacking on three flanks, according to my scout's report. Gloucester, York and Hastings against Somerset, Wenlock and Devonshire. Clarence rides with his brother Edward, and my son is with Wenlock. Brother-in-law against brother-in-law! Cousin against cousin! Your father and your uncle dead! So it goes on.'

'I wish there could be an end of it,' Anne said.

'Today we will make an end,' the Queen said grimly.

'We'll have three Yorkist heads to grace the towers of Tewkesbury.'

Edward, George, Richard. She saw each one in her mind and closed her eyes briefly. It no longer mattered who lost as long as Richard was not killed or captured.

'If only the Welsh would come! Their advance cannot have been cut off,' the Queen was fretting. 'I've a mind to ride out and discover matters for myself!'

'Madam, we have to wait! You said that it was the task of women to wait,' Anne said quickly.

'I have been mother and father to my son these many years past,' her mother-in-law said. 'His Grace King Henry is not — not always himself, I fear. I have been lioness when once I was kitten, and I trust nobody, not even you, my little Anne Neville. You and Gloucester were once playmates, so they tell me?'

'At Middleham, Your Grace, but it was long ago.'

Long ago, when I was young and ate sugared almonds on the stair.

'I wish someone would come,' the Queen muttered, resuming her restless pacing.

The day wore on, made more frustrating by the sounds of battle that faintly penetrated the thick walls of the convent. A nun brought food, and water for washing, and once a scout, blood running down his face, staggered into the outer enclosure to call through the grille that the Welsh had not arrived.

'Your Grace, you ought to rest,' Anne pleaded, but the Queen turned upon her, crying fiercely,

'Time to rest when we have news of victory!'

'There are horsemen coming!' Anne's

ears, sharpened by anxiety, caught the clip-clop of hoofs.

'Let us receive them.' The Queen, her face ravaged by the long hours of waiting, stood with her cloak flung about her and her eyes fixed upon the door.

There was the indignant squeal of a nun in the corridor beyond as she protested,

'Sirs, this enclosure is forbidden to men.'

A deeper voice answered. A door banged. Somewhere in the gathering gloom a torch blazed against the sky. Dear Lord! whoever wins let not Gloucester perish!

The man who entered was a stranger to her, but she disliked the gloating triumph on his face even as he spoke.

'Margaret of Anjou? I, Sir William Stanley, bring you tidings of a great victory won by His Grace King Edward against his enemies, and am empowered to take you and your companion in crime into custody as prisoners of the state.'

'My son?' She mouthed the words shiveringly.

'Edward of Lancaster is dead,' Sir William said bluntly, his smile widening. 'He was in full flight towards the Avon when the Duke of Clarence struck him down. Milords Wenlock and Courtenay were slain in the fray and Somerset was taken from the abbey where he had sought refuge and executed less than an hour since. Your son is dead, madam, and the rebellion over.'

There was a pause that lasted the length of a heartbeat and then the Queen threw back her head and screamed over and over until the whole world seemed filled with the sounds of agony.

A week later the triumphal procession entered London. The last flickers of rebellion had been quenched and every citizen was a fervent Yorkist. At the head of the procession King

Edward was flanked by his brothers of Clarence and Gloucester, purple cloaks over their armour, banners of white and gold carried before them. They rode slowly, gravely acknowledging the cheers, the noise of cannon being discharged across the river, the flags and fluttering ribbons strung across the streets. Knights, close packed in ranks of steel, squires in the liveries of York, Clarence and Gloucester, and Essex, page-boys in feathered caps and short cloaks, girls throwing flowers, halberdiers marching with fixed pikes, archers with their quivers slung upon their backs, all passed in a blur of colour and noise.

The King's Woodville wife, newly come from Sanctuary, rode in a carriage lined with cloth of silver, her three little daughters riding with her, the baby Prince borne by his nurse followed in the next carriage, and behind them Isobel, Duchess of Clarence, diamonds winking at her throat, rode on a horse caparisoned in blue and gold.

Priests followed, vestments of scarlet, copes stiff with gold and silver, and choirboys singing as they came, though their treble voices were scarcely audible above the general hubbub.

On they came, in wave after wave of colour and splendour, and at the last, in a sable-draped carriage two figures draped in black. Margaret of Anjou and Anne of Warwick sitting together while, ahead of them, spiked on poles, the rotting heads of Prince Edward and Somerset were borne aloft.

Anne held herself erect, her eyes lowered, for, if she raised them she would vomit again. Her face was so white that it stood out against the background of her wide hood as if she, too, had been executed. At her side Queen Margaret was stiff as a waxen idol, her face a heavily painted mask, only her eyes bright and unseeing as she gazed ahead.

The crowds pressing forward fell uneasily silent as the prisoners passed.

It was only right that traitors should be punished, but the wife of King Henry was a woman of great courage, and Warwick's daughter a mere girl of 15 used as a pawn in the deadly game of chess between York and Lancaster. Out of the silence came murmurs of sympathy. A few women wept and a boy, running from the side and ducking between the guards, threw a posy of violets into her lap. She held them to her nose, breathing in the sweet, musky perfume, praying that she would get through this nightmare without breaking down.

She had seen Richard from a distance but he had taken no notice of her. He had been named Constable of all England, and a retinue of attendants had surrounded him.

The carriage was swinging out of the main procession, the cheers diminishing as it rattled into a side street. Anne cautiously raised her head and saw the grisly trophies had gone. Ahead of her was the handsome façade of a great mansion and she blinked uncertainly.

'Anne! Little Lady Anne!' The voice was as familiar as her own and red curls flew wildly from beneath the lace coif.

'Ankarette? *Ankarette!*' A flood of relief engulfed her as she sat, tears loosed from her burning eyes, and then the carriage rolled to a halt and one of the archers was lifting her down and Ankarette was hugging her tightly and the fear was lifting like all the nightmares of childhood.

8

It was a mild September as if, after the disorders of the previous year, the gods of the elements had decided to bring a gentle autumn to cool passions and soothe the wounds of the summer.

At Crosby Place Anne lived retired, her nerves slowly strengthening after the horrors of Tewkesbury. Her apartment was a large and comfortable one and she seldom left it save to walk in the pleached alleys at the side of the great house. The mansion backed on to the river and from her window she could see the numerous boats ferrying up and down the swift flowing water. Many of the boats bore coats-of-arms and she amused herself by identifying the various officials on the King's business.

It was as if Edward had never been away. The life of the city moved on, it seemed, no matter who sat upon the throne. Poor Henry of Lancaster had died on the very night of the Yorkist's triumphant return to his capital. Officially it had been given out that His Grace had died of displeasure, but others whispered of a darker end. Queen Margaret had been taken to Wellington Manor to await the arrival of her ransom from France, and Anne's uncle, the Archbishop, had been exiled to Calais. Of her mother she had heard only that the Countess was still in the Sanctuary of Beaulieu, having been deprived of her estates.

Crosby Place was the London home of Cecily Neville, the King's mother, and it was thus a suitable place for Anne to be lodged. The Dowager Duchess had been one of the great beauties of her day and her marriage had been a love match. Now she was in her mid-fifties but still a handsome woman, her eyes keen under her bands of coiled grey hair, her manner imperious. She had greeted Anne kindly enough, but her voice was too commanding, her smile edged with indifference. The girl preferred the seclusion of her own quarters where she could almost imagine herself back in the nursery at Middleham with Ankarette knitting away by the fire.

'My poor husband died of the sweat nearly a year ago,' she had told Anne, 'so I was free to come back into service for a little while until you are settled.'

'Settled? Where settled?' Anne asked bleakly. 'I am a prisoner.'

'A formality!' Ankarette flapped her hands. 'There are happier days in store for you, my loveling.'

Anne could not look ahead so far. In dreams she saw the prince's head spiked to the long pole and the mouth opened, saying 'Kiss me, wife,' and then she heard the insane screaming of the bereaved and broken Queen. By day she kept Ankarette close by her, making the woman go over and over the little unimportant details of her married life as if, by learning about them, she could dull the recent terrible events in her own life.

She had gone down into the alley one afternoon to pace slowly up and down the flagstoned paths with their borders of shells. It was peaceful here with nothing but the chiming of bells from nearby steeples to remind her that she was in the heart of London.

'Anne? Anne, are you there?' The voice intruded upon her tranquillity and she jumped nervously as her sister's feet tapped briskly towards her.

Isobel had grown prettier than ever, Anne thought with a twinge of envy. Her eyes were sky blue and her skin had the bloom of a fresh peach.

'Always mooning about,' Isobel said now, pausing to shake her head at her younger sister. 'George is here from Court with news for you.'

'Has something happened? Our lady mother?'

'Is well, according to her last letter. Do hurry, Anne. This is important.'

Anne could think of nothing to

interest her, but she obediently followed the older girl up the steps into the tapestry-hung solar. The Duke of Clarence, his handsome face pulled into lines of gravity, came forward and took her hands, his voice low and urgent.

'Anne, I have come as quickly as possible to warn you. I slipped away from Council, but I may soon be called back to my attendance there.'

'Warn me of what?' She pulled her hands away, wishing that it were possible for her to meet George without remembering that he was the one who had struck down poor, spoilt Ned.

'My brother of Gloucester has asked His Grace for permission to wed you,' he said.

Wild joy bubbled up in her. He had not forgotten their plighted troth after all. He had remained true to their compact.

'Anne, you are in the gravest danger,' Isobel said, drawing her sister to a chair.

'Danger? To be married is a danger?'

'To wed Richard of Gloucester would mean your death,' Isobel said.

'I'll not believe that! Richard would never hurt me,' Anne said. She was beginning to tremble but she set her jaw firmly.

'Has he once visited you or written to you since you were brought into London?' George demanded.

'I heard that he went into the northern counties,' Anne said.

'And since his return he has been most industriously inquiring into your fortune,' he told her.

'My fortune?' She stared at him uncomprehendingly.

'Our father died an attainted rebel and his lands were forfeit to the crown,' her sister explained, 'but our lady mother had property in her own right. She was deprived of that.'

'I know. The King — .'

'The King has just decreed that the property of the Countess of Warwick be given to the husbands of her daughters.

Isobel and I are already married, but you are a widow. My little brother was very eager to offer for your hand once he had that information.'

'It can't be true.' She had begun to shake more violently, her nails digging into her palms and leaving bright crescents of blood. 'Milord of Gloucester would never seek to marry me for my mother's lands!'

'That is precisely what Milord of Gloucester seeks to do,' George said.

'If that were all.' Isobel shuddered, her lovely face paling.

'M-Most marriages are affairs of property,' Anne said, reverting to a childish stammer that she had long since managed to control.

'My brother of Gloucester has another bride in mind. Mary of Burgundy is the greatest prize in Europe,' George said.

'No! He'd not want to marry Mary of Burgundy,' Anne said. 'You said that he wished to marry me! He cannot wed us both!'

'He will marry you in order to secure your share of our mother's money,' Isobel said.

'And when you are gone he will wed Mary of Burgundy,' George said.

'Gone where? Where am I going?' Anne asked in bewilderment.

'He will rid himself of you,' George said. 'God forgive me for such a thought, but it would be so easy to arrange an accident.'

'He is not capable of such a deed,' Anne said.

Anger was rising in her and her voice came out strong and clear.

'Who do you think rid the realm of King Henry?' George asked.

'I cannot — it has nothing to do with the case,' she protested.

'You think Richard a perfect, gentle knight? He's young, I know, but he has experience of death.'

'In battle, yes.'

'My brother Edward gave Richard a private mission on the very day we came back to London,' George said.

'His mission was at the Tower, and he was admitted there with four other gentlemen of his suite. They went to the apartment where the witless King was confined. The next day his death was announced.'

'King Henry's death was a political necessity,' Isobel said with an air of gentleness, 'but Richard carried out the deed in person, to prove his continued loyalty. He is capable of a private murder, Anne.'

'But not of me! Not of *me*!' She leapt up, twisting away from them, her hands outstretched to ward them away. 'He loves me! Ever since — since we were children he has loved me.'

'You forget the children he has sired!' George said. 'He is not yet 19 and he has not even tried to be true to you.'

'I know about the babe, K-Katherine. The sewing maid, Molly. He said it meant nothing, that it was the impulse of an hour. We swore to wait for each other. Loyalty binds me. He made it his motto.'

'Loyalty to the King!' George seized her hands, pulling her against him. 'Anne, wake up! You'll be 16 on your next birthday, not six! Your childhood is over and you have to stop dreaming. Richard is loyal to Edward and to himself. Not to you, Anne! He never stopped seeing that girl! She went with him to Burgundy and a month ago she bore him a second child, only a 12 month after the first.'

'A son who is named John,' Isobel said. 'Molly and the children are at Sheriff Hutton. He has never been faithful to you, Anne. He will wed you for your lands and when you are dead he will wed Mary of Burgundy. You must wake up, Anne!'

The waking was bitter. Staring at them she knew that they spoke the truth. Molly had given birth to a second child, and that made Richard's word to her valueless. He had never written to her, never come to see her, never loved her for a moment. And now, because of her share of her mother's fortune, he planned to marry her. Rich maid, poor maid, beggar maid — yes, that described her exactly.

'There is a boat with Richard's crest upon it landing at the water-gate,' Isobel said in accents of sudden terror.

'Anne, go to your chamber. I'll make excuse that you're not here,' George said swiftly.

'Perhaps if I refused him myself — ,' she began.

'Go up to the gallery. You can both see and hear from there and come down or not as you please,' he suggested.

Anne gathered up her skirts and fled up the stairs that led to the long gallery above. There was a spyhole cut in the panelled wall, placed there by some former owner of the house when the solar had been used as a servant's hall. She stood by it now, her eye to the crack, her heart hammering beneath her stiff bodice.

Below she could see George of Clarence, his blond head thrown back,

Isobel at his side and then, facing them, the shorter, slighter figure of Gloucester.

'Brother, God give you greeting,' George said.

'And you too,' came Richard's voice. 'You left the Council so quickly that I feared illness.'

'I was anxious to get home to my wife?'

'Is my own betrothed here?' Richard asked.

'Mary of Burgundy is in her father's kingdom.'

'I refer to the Lady Anne Neville. The marriage with Burgundy was His Grace's notion, to strengthen the treaty.'

'The Lady Anne is not for you,' George said, his voice rising slightly. 'She was placed in my ward.'

'In our lady mother's.'

'And as she is at Court for a few days the Lady Anne is under my protection.'

'She can be transferred to mine,' Richard said, still calmly. 'You will kindly inform her that I am here.'

'This is my private house, brother!' George snapped. 'Don't trouble to give me orders on my own property!'

'You cannot see my sister or take her away with you!' Isobel gasped out.

'I intend to marry her and see her take her rightful place at Court,' Richard said.

Through the spyhole she could see his narrow face set in hard, unrelenting lines. His voice was still quiet but it was lined with steel, and his thin hand was clenched upon the hilt of his sword.

'The Lady Anne is not for you,' George said loudly.

'That's for me to decide and for His Grace to approve,' Richard said obstinately.

'Then run back to our royal brother and tell him that now I am the Lady Anne's guardian and forbid the marriage,' George said angrily.

'I will tell him so, and then I will return,' Richard said.

The slight figure bowed and moved

out of her field of vision. For a moment she had an insane impulse to run back along the corridor and down the stairs and into his arms, crying out that she loved him even if he had betrayed her.

Cold and sick, she leaned her head against the panel and tried not to remember the clear-eyed boy who had given her sugared almonds and sat with her in the old nursery at Middleham. Her father had been a great and powerful man but he had changed his coat to suit his personal ambition just as George had done. She had been a fool to believe that one man could remain true when all the rest of the world was false.

'I know my brother!' The Duke of Clarence was hurrying towards her. 'He will be back within the hour with a search warrant. Nothing will turn Richard from his stated purpose.'

'What are we to do?' Isobel wailed, hard on his heels.

'We must hide her somewhere.' George put his arm about Anne and chewed his lip thoughtfully.

'Cannot she go north to Middleham?' Isobel asked.

'That would be the first place he would search,' her husband said sensibly.

'Calais? Or could she go into France?'

'He would look there too. Richard will look everywhere.'

'Then you had best hand me over at once and let me take my chance!' Anne said despairingly.

'You need not hide for ever. Richard will be forced to marry elsewhere within a year or two if you are not to be found. I will put my own efforts to that end,' George told her. 'Once my brother is safely wed then you can return.'

'Return from where? Where am I to go?' Anne looked desperately from one face to the next.

'To a place my brother would never think of seeking you,' George said.

'There is no such place,' Anne began,

but the Duke interrupted her, snapping his fingers in triumph.

'My brother will expect you to lie hid in some castle or fortress,' he said. 'He will have his men rake through every stronghold in the kingdom. I tell you we have to hide you in some place where nobody would dream of going to find you.'

'Is there such a place?' She looked up at him imploringly.

'There is an inn in St Martin's Lane, near to the Sanctuary.'

'Could she not go into Sanctuary?' Isobel asked.

'In his present mood Richard is quite capable of violating Sanctuary,' George frowned. 'No, Anne shall go to the inn — not as a guest but as a servant-girl.'

'A servant-girl! Husband, you must be out of your mind!' Isobel gasped. 'A Neville to be a servant! I never heard of such a thing!'

'And neither, I'll warrant you, has my brother of Gloucester,' George said. 'It is the perfect plan. Perfect!

The inn is a respectable place, and you'll not be recognised. Why should you be? You have been seen in public only once since you came to the city and that was four months ago. You will be safer than you would be in any castle or manor.'

'Ankarette will be very shocked,' Anne began doubtfully.

'Ankarette mustn't know. Nobody is to know except the three of us,' he said swiftly.

'Her manner of speech will betray her,' Isobel frowned. 'The way that she walks and talks and eats — all these will betray her.'

'She can be a dumb maid,' George said. 'The daughter of a poor knight slain at Tewkesbury and left friendless. Gently bred but now penniless and glad of honest work. Isobel, can you get hold of a plain kirtle and bodice and a pair of unpiked shoes?'

'I'll get them now,' Isobel said promptly.

'We'll have you away before anyone is

aware you are not in the house,' George said.

His arm was still about her, his voice comforting. Tears sprang to her eyes as she choked out,

'Why did you leave my lord father and return to the King?'

'Because, at the last, I could not bring myself to fight against my own brother,' he said sadly. 'I know that it meant deserting my own wife's father, and my cousin too. I know that, but Edward is closer kin.'

'And even if my lord father had won the battle you would not have been made King,' she thought, and began to cry softly because she could no longer trust anyone properly.

'I found some clothes in the linen closet,' Isobel panted out, returning. 'You had better come quickly to our bedchamber.'

Twenty minutes later two ill-assorted figures made their way through a side door into the network of streets and squares beyond. The Duke was clad in a plain cloak and wide-brimmed hat and at his side trotted a small maidservant, her hair braided under a neat white coif, her ankle-length kirtle and hodded cape betokening a modest and respectable girl. This was the first time in her life that Anne had gone on foot through the public streets, and her first impression was of noise and bustle. She had not realised before how common folk hurried along, not bothering to step aside as a horseman or lumbering dray-cart went by.

The buildings seemed to be crammed together with no space for their occupants to breathe and the smell from the gutters made her want to retch. The cries of street hawkers peddling their wares mingled with the ringing of bells from the numerous churches, the clopping of hooves along the cobbled roads, the rattling of harness as a troop of archers swaggered by. Nobody took the slightest notice of her, a circumstance so unusual that after ten minutes walking she felt her nervousness begin to ebb away. Before she had always ridden in saddle or litter and people, pointing her out, had commented audibly on the 'little Warwick girl'. Now it was as if she were invisible, with nobody to spare her more than a passing glance.

The Duke seemed to know his way without asking and the thought crossed her mind that he was probably used to roistering in the taverns or attending the various cockfights and bull-baitings held in the city. There were patches of green even within these walls. Trees drooped their autumn heads in the gardens of some of the larger stone dwellings and on a space no bigger than a small room a tethered cow munched contentedly.

'Remember to be dumb,' George warned her as they continued along their way.

She nodded, looking round her with increasing interest. Nobody, she thought, would be able to find just one person in this vast rabbit warren.

'My mother will be anxious when she learns that I'm gone,' she said aloud.

'Isobel will tell her that you are safe in Sanctuary,' he assured her.

'And you will send word when it is safe for me to reveal myself?'

'Richard will have to marry elsewhere eventually and His Grace will be eager for a new foreign alliance, even if it is not with Burgundy,' the Duke said.

A marriage made for reasons of state was not likely to be a love match. Anne remembered the girl, Molly, with her two children. It was the serving-maid to whom Richard had given his affections. He had no motive save greed for marrying the Countess of Warwick's daughter.

'That is the inn just ahead,' the Duke pointed. 'The host knows me well, and will accept you at face value. John Ball is an honest man but not the greatest brain in London!' He pressed her hand encouragingly and then strode on briskly into a yard noisy with horses and dogs, calling as he went, 'Master

Ball! Master Ball! Are you dead or clapped into the Fleet?'

'My lord Duke, I give you greeting!' A burly, red-faced man, who looked as if he sampled his own wares extensively, hurried out and bent the knee with immense pleasure beaming out of his eyes.

'I have a favour to ask you,' George said motioning the other to rise.

'Anything milord wants — but milord comes without escort! Something is wrong?'

'Nothing in the world,' the Duke assured him. 'I count my brother so safe upon the throne that I roam the streets of his capital without fear. 'Tis this little maid that I'm here about.'

'Your leman, sir?' The landlord gave Anne a glance which said plainly he didn't think much of the Duke's taste.

'My entire devotion is to my lady wife,' George said frowning. 'This maid is Ankarette Hutton. Her father was a tenant of mine, but he was killed at Tewkesbury and his property forfeit.

His daughter needs employment.'

'Why not in Your Lordship's house?' Master Ball inquired.

'Her father fought for the Anjou queen despite being my tenant,' George said, 'and I am not anxious to have the daughters of rebels in my household. Can you find employment for her? She was gently bred and is not used to scullion work.'

'My wife is at market,' the landlord said, 'but she'll take the lass in, I've no doubt.'

'There's one other thing.' George lowered his voice, taking the other by the arm. 'The poor child is a mute. She has not spoken a word since birth, not one word!'

'Mute? Poor soul!' The landlord looked at her with sympathy.

'I'd not have her teased nor put upon by the other servants,' George said.

'Your Lordship may rely on me,' Master Ball said, turning to Anne and raising his voice. 'Missy, you come with me now and we'll find you a place to sleep and some work.'

'She is dumb, not deaf,' George said, looking amused.

'You'll stay for something to eat, sir? We don't see sufficient of you these days.'

'I am expected back at once. Family matters. I will look in from time to time to see how the maid does. Can you spare me one of your lads to hail me a boat back?'

'Of course, sir. Ah! here's Jeannie now. Pardon me, sir.'

Master Ball hastened to the outer gate to greet a plump matron in an immensely wide hennin who sank to her knees at the sight of the Duke.

'Get up, get up, Mistress Ball. Stand on no ceremony in your own yard!' George exclaimed heartily. 'I've brought you a new servant-girl.'

'A poor dumb soul,' her husband said. 'Name of Ankarette — Hutton? Her father died at Tewkesbury and she needs employment.'

'She's very small,' Mistress Ball said doubtfully.

'Past 15 and very bright and willing,' the Duke assured her.

'Well, she cannot serve in the bar,' the good lady said doubtfully. 'What work can she do?'

'Cooking,' the Duke said promptly. 'She makes fine, light bread.'

Anne, opening her own mouth in horror, closed it again as Mistress Ball turned towards her.

'If Milord of Clarence will excuse us, I'll take you indoors, Ankarette,' she said pleasantly.

'Be sure that I will recommend your hostelry,' the Duke said, giving her his most charming smile. 'Be a good maid, Ankarette.'

'Where are your wits, missy? Make your curtsy to the Duke!' Master Ball said looking scandalised.

Anne, who had started to hold out her hand, hastily bent her knee.

A few minutes later she was being ushered into a tiny chamber under the eaves of the inn. A pallet on the floor, a low table with a jug and ewer on it comprised the only furniture, and there was no window save for a narrow skylight.

'My last girl left to get wed a week since,' Mistress Ball said, 'and I've been run off my feet ever since. I've been hoping for a nice young girl to train up as a cook maid. Where are your things?'

Anne looked at her blankly.

'Another kirtle, apron, a Sunday bodice?' the landlord's wife said. 'Did you bring nothing with you at all?'

Anne shook her head.

'Well, we'll have to see what can be done, I suppose! You don't look strong, so we'll not expect too much,' Mistress Ball said. 'We start the baking at six, so that most of it can be cleared by mid-afternoon, and you will be free in the evenings save for clearing away at the last. I pay bed and board and a shilling a week.'

Anne nodded again, and the other gave her a frowning look before she turned and went down the narrow stairway.

The Duke had gone and Master Ball was jangling a pouch of silver.

'Milord of Clarence is generous,' he said.

'John, that girl is no knight's daughter,' his wife said. 'Her nails are polished pink and her hair smells of perfume. Who is she?'

'As far as we're concerned her name is Ankarette Hutton and she's working here as a cook maid,' the landlord said. 'Not our place to inquire any further, not where the Duke is concerned in the business.'

'And dumb? She's no more dumb than you or I are,' his wife insisted. 'She opened her mouth to answer me until she remembered to shut it again!'

'It's the Duke's business,' he repeated.

'Aye.' She reached over and weighed the bag thoughtfully in her hand. 'And the Duke is generous to those who know how to keep their mouths shut, eh?'

'Keep your eye on the little missy,' her husband advised. 'She will need a friend one day perhaps, but we'd do well to remember that Milord of Clarence is our patron.'

'I'll remember that,' she said stolidly.

Up in the tiny attic room Anne stood on tiptoe in a vain attempt to look out of the skylight, but could see nothing except a smoky sky. Quite suddenly her horizons were limited to four walls of wattle and daub and a narrow doorway that led to the stairs. Narrow but safe from the treacheries of the Court and the betrayal of those who she believed had loved her.

9

Anne had slipped away from her duties
for an hour to watch a procession on its
way down river. This was a day of
celebration to mark the birth of King
Edward's fifth child and fourth daughter, born at Windsor a few days before.
The royal household was on its way to
the Tower, where there was to be a
banquet before they proceeded to
Windsor to inspect the little Lady
Margaret.

'Not that they'll rejoice long,' a
woman among the crowd at the water's
edge said with gloomy satisfaction. '
'Tis said the babe is sickly.'

'Well, he's sired plenty of healthy
ones in and out of holy wedlock,' a man
remarked. 'There go the royal children
now! God bless 'em all, I say! Lady
Bess, Lady Mary, Lady Cecily and little
Prince Ned!'

But Prince Ned was dead, Anne thought, his head spiked upon a pole. She wanted no part of the chubby, fair-haired baby in his nurse's arms or the three little girls in their elaborate robes who stood at the rail of the brightly painted barge. Their royal father stood with them, acknowledging the cheers from the banks. A florid, handsome King, who had already crowded more into his 30 years than most men did in a lifetime, he was popular with the Londoners for his trading policies, the firm hand with which he had ended the Lancastrian menace, the generosity of his response to the merchants's wives who offered him kisses in exchange for financial benefices which their husbands paid. They could almost forgive his marriage to a Woodville who, for all her low connections, had proved a good wife and shown her excellent sense by retreating into Sanctuary when danger threatened instead of dashing about on horseback with an army as Margaret of

Anjou had done.

'There goes Milord of Clarence and the Gloucester Duke!' another shrilled. 'There has been a reconciliation between them.'

'I did not know,' Anne said carefully, 'that they had quarrelled.'

'Oh, aye, Mistress. Year before last, Milord of Gloucester wanted to wed Lady Anne Neville, she whom they married off to the Lancaster prince. Milord Clarence wouldn't have it so, not when it meant he had to share half his own wife's fortune with his brother! So Lady Anne vanished and it's my belief she's dead, poor soul.'

'But you say they are reconciled?' She pulled timidly at the man's sleeve, her eyes still following the two figures who stood in the boat, under canopies painted with lilies and leopards and the white boar of Gloucester. There was such a pain at her heart that it was difficult to speak.

'What? Oh, yes, reconciled! After a fashion only for the Lady Anne is still missing. They do say Richard of Gloucester has agreed to forfeit all the lands he would have had save Middleham and Sheriff Hutton. Mind! he still has to find his bride, for Clarence declares he does not know where she is.'

So it was not her fortune that Richard had desired, and he had not gone off to marry a foreign princess. In those things at least, George had been mistaken. Her pain increased, and she blinked to hold back the tears. Whatever had happened was no longer any concern of hers. For the past 18 months she had been Ankarette Hutton, cook maid. The months had wrought a change in her. Now she ventured out frequently, dropping occasionally into brief conversations with people, carefully roughening her accent. Within the tavern she had succeeded in keeping silent, though there were many times when she longed to answer back the servants' teasing. The work was not hard, but the hours were long, and in the early weeks she had burned more bread than she had baked. Now she was much more proficient and found a certain satisfaction in well-risen loaves, but in the long evenings when she sat in her tiny attic room and heard the sounds of revelry drifting up from the bar below a sense of complete desolation stole over her. There had been no message from Crosby Place, and she had no means of getting word to anyone even if she had dared.

There was no happiness in her existence now, but there was a certain freedom. She could go out without fear of being recognised, and there was safety in her little room such as she had known only in childhood when she had not met greed or treachery.

The procession was almost out of sight, and she had no heart to watch it further. She turned and pushed back through the crowds, thinking wryly that the common folk stank less than they had done when she had first mingled with them. It was wiser to think of things like that than to remember the slight figure in green and gold who had stood with George in the barge as it glided down river.

She was a trifle breathless by the time she reached the inn and, leaning to catch her breath, wondered suddenly if George of Clarence had hoped that she might fall sick and die. There was no reason why she should remain in hiding if Richard was willing to give up his share of her mother's estates. George had been less than honest with her just as he had been less than honest with her father.

It made no matter. Richard and she were parted and nothing could possibly bring back what had once lain between them. Wearily she straightened her aching shoulders and went into the tavern, ducking her head according to her habit. She was so familiar a figure by now that few gave her more than a casual glance, and in a few moments she was kneading dough in a corner of the warm kitchen, a white apron covering her neat dress and her braided hair tied back into a scarf.

Beyond the kitchen came the cheerful clatter of mugs and goblets and the gushing of ale from the barrels. The regular customers were arriving, many of them still chatting about the glories of the procession. The laughter ebbed and flowed, reaching every corner of the cheerful hostelry. The spit boy, who was weak in the head, joined in, giggling at what he couldn't understand, and she went over and gave him a biscuit.

There was a tapping at the side door and she stepped across to open it, and stood back, her face blank with shock.

Richard stood there, a dark cloak wrapped about him, a jewel gleaming on his forefinger as he raised his hand and caught at her wrist. In his face his eyes were darkly slanting and he was poised like a cat on the balls of his feet. She thought wildly that she was the mouse, caught in the fascination of the hunter's snare.

'It has taken me a long time to find you,' he said, as coolly as if they had been parted the previous day. 'You must have been anxious to avoid marriage with me. Get your cloak.'

'I have my work to do,' she said gaspingly.

'The work can wait. You have other matters to attend,' Richard informed her. 'Get your cloak and come with me.'

'I'm not going anywhere,' she began quaveringly.

'Unless you want to be carried,' he said, black brows twitching.

Her cloak was over a stool. Her eyes flickered to it and the Duke reached for it, wrapping it about her shoulders.

'I'll not come,' she said, but he was already thrusting her none too gently into the alley.

'Ankarette is waiting for you in the Sanctuary of St Martin,' he said, hurrying her over the cobbles.

'Ankarette!'

'It was thanks to her that you were

221

found at all,' he informed her curtly. 'She never believed that fairy-tale of your having fled to the Continent, not when all your clothes had been left behind. She said nothing but she watched and waited, the last summer when the linen was laundered and checked one of the maids complained that some of her garments were missing. After that she was concerned to discover your whereabouts. It meant long and painstaking inquiries but in the end we discovered you. It was not very imaginative of my brother to choose the name of 'Ankarette' for you, or to insist upon you being mute. You must have been out of your mind to agree to such a scheme!'

'I will not be rushed into marriage with a man who cares nothing for me,' she interrupted.

'Nobody is going to force you into anything,' he said impatiently. 'Here is the Sanctuary gate. I've made the necessary preparations for your reception, and Ankarette has brought one of your own dresses. It would not be fitting for the daughter of Warwick to get married in an apron.'

'I am not going to marry you,' she said feebly, but he was ushering her through a spiked gate and up a twisting stair to a low chamber where a fire burned brightly and Ankarette rushed to enfold her in a comforting and garrulous embrace.

'You naughty girl! To run off and hide yourself away without one word! I have never been so fretted in all my life, never! And what is that on your hands?'

'Flour,' Anne said, not knowing whether to laugh or cry.

'Your Ladyship must have a good wash and change your garments. Give us half an hour, sir Duke,' Ankarette fussed.

'Twenty minutes,' Richard said and quitted the room.

'Lord help us, but your nails are ruined!' Ankarette wailed, 'and what possessed you to venture out with an apron on? I shall sink into my grave if anyone recognised you! Now let me unbraid your hair. A bride should wear her hair loose and shining.'

'I am not going to be a bride,' Anne protested, submitting to her nurse's ministrations.

'Hush now, do, and get your hands into this hot, soapy water!' Ankarette retorted.

Before the 20 minutes were up she was attired in a gown of cream silk, its hanging sleeves encrusted with gold, her hair brushed out to fall to her waist in a darkly gleaming mass.

'Is she fit to be seen?' Richard inquired, tapping on the door and putting his head in.

'Pretty as a picture,' Ankarette said.

'Leave us, then. We will see you in the chapel.' He held open the door for her and closed it softly as she went through.

'Chapel? I'm going to no chapel,' Anne began.

'We are going into the chapel to be married,' Richard said calmly.

'I will not wed you,' she said, backing

away from him towards the window. 'I am resolved to wed nobody ever again.'

'Was Edward of Lancaster so loving a lord?' he asked in sudden mockery.

'Edward of Lancaster never touched me,' she flashed, and bit her lip.

'So! You are still my betrothed, then.' For the first time he smiled slightly.

'I am nobody's betrothed!' she snapped. 'I am a — .'

'A cook maid, it seems! Oh, Anne, Anne!' He stepped quickly to her, seizing her hands. 'Anne, you are a royal lady, heiress to one of the noblest families in the kingdom! You cannot throw it all away to live dumbly in a kitchen! You cannot!'

'If I must go back then let me join my lady mother in Sanctuary,' she begged.

'You will marry me here privately and in the morning we will travel north to Middleham.'

'Is it true that you gave nearly all the lands of mine due to your brother of Clarence?' she asked.

'Except for Middleham and Sheriff Hutton. I have fortune sufficient for us both and never needed your share,' he said quickly. 'But Middleham is our own private place.'

'And Sheriff Hutton is within easy travelling distance of Middleham,' she gibed. 'Your sewing-maid mistress and her two bastards are there, aren't they?'

'Yes. The children are there,' he said without expression.

'And the girl, Molly?'

'She is to be wed to a respectable merchant in a few months' time. I paid her dowry, and in return she leaves the children in my care.'

'Are you fond of them?'

'Of course I am fond of them!' He dropped her hands and spoke roughly. 'They are my own flesh and blood! Katherine and John, my children. I will have them reared and educated as befits their station.'

'And their mother?'

'Pleasured me well, but is soon to be wed. So you need have no jealousy. A bachelor has the right to take a woman, but a husband — .'

'Has one ready for his use at home, I suppose? No, my lord! You must look elsewhere for a wife,' she interrupted.

'Since we were children it was agreed between us without words that we would marry. We needed no words then,' he said sombrely. 'What has changed you? Is it because of Molly? Are you so hard that you begrudge me the favours of a girl who never harmed you and only gave me a few hours of respite from the loneliness of not being with you.'

'King Henry was murdered,' she said chokingly. 'Poor, innocent man, done to death in the Tower! Oh, you will tell me that his death was a political necessity! But had you need to carry out the deed yourself!'

'I went in with the King's warrant to the Tower,' he said. 'I never raised my hand to join in the act.'

'But you witnessed it?'

'As the King's witness,' he nodded.

'So did others. Poor Henry was given drugged wine with his supper and then his skull cleaved by an axe. He felt nothing, knew no fear.'

'And now the Court makes merry in that same Tower!'

'I left the banquet to come to you.'

'Then you might have spared yourself the trouble,' she said bitterly.

'I have the marriage licence and the priest is waiting,' Richard said.

'I'll not go to the chapel,' she said stubbornly. 'You may have me dragged up the aisle but I'll not speak the words. A bride must go consenting.'

'And must give reasons for not consenting,' he argued. 'What reasons have you for refusing?'

'I have no mind to wed.' She tore her gaze from his own darkly compelling stare and forced lightness into her voice. 'I wish to be taken to the Sanctuary at Beaulieu, or to the household of my sister.'

'To live as a dependent relative with my brother of Clarence? You were framed for marriage, Anne. The King consents to our private marriage and to our taking up residence at Middleham. Would you not like to see Middleham again? We could be peaceful there, away from the glitter of the Court.'

'I liked being a cook maid,' she said.

'God save us! you may provide all Yorkshire with bread if you wish, once we are wed and living there,' he exclaimed. 'Anne, use your sense! If you remain unwed you remain without adequate protection against those who seek to use you for their own ends.'

Her resolution was faltering. The dress she wore, the size and comfort of the room in which they stood, all served to remind her of the mode of living on which she had turned her back. She had almost forgotten how it was to wear pretty garments and sleep in a curtained bed.

'I saw the river procession this afternoon,' she said. 'I stood among the crowds on the bank and watched the state barges go past towards the Tower.'

'I never thought of anyone save you as we sailed down the river,' he said slowly. 'I feared that the information Ankarette obtained had been false, or that the others might have learned it and spirited you away again. I had kept my plans to myself. Only the King knows it. Oh, George probably guesses. I found it difficult to contain my joy when I knew where you were hidden.'

'And now that I am found? How do you feel now?' she asked.

'I would like to put you across my knee,' he said curtly, 'but attacking women is not the act of a gallant duke. So I will marry you and pray to make you so content that you cease running away every time my back is turned.'

He had taken her hand again, and his smile was the crooked smile of the boy she had known, and the doubts and the fears were stilled. She let her hand rest in his and he led her, unresistingly, out of the chamber and along a silent, echoing corridor.

'The priest grows impatient,' Ankarette said, hurrying towards them.

'The bride needed a little persuasion,' Richard said. 'Take your place in the chapel.'

'Lady Anne, you have neither veil nor flowers,' Ankarette exclaimed.

'She needs none,' he said.

'But the ring? Did your lordship remember to obtain a wedding-ring?'

'I have it here. Get to your place now.'

'All happiness, Lady Anne.' Ankarette bobbed a curtsy and went down the stairs ahead of them.

'She will travel back to her husband's old home with a handsome pension from me,' Richard said. 'It is best for her to live independently. Come, we'd better not keep the priest waiting any longer.'

She went meekly, her own inclination banishing the last fragments of distrust.

The chapel was small and dimly lit by tall wax candles. There were several people present but she never afterwards remembered their faces or learned their names. The priest had a gentle voice and showed no sign of the impatience that had been attributed to him.

The ceremony seemed very brief, her own voice faltering, her hand cold in Richard's warm clasp. His voice was firm and clear, ringing through the stone chamber in triumph. He sounded as if he had just won a victory, she thought.

They knelt for the final blessing and then they were walking together down the short aisle, with the incense spiralling in the air and murmurs of congratulation from those assembled.

'We ride north at dawn,' he said, putting his arm about her as they went up the staircase.

'To Middleham?' She looked at him hopefully.

'I promised you so.'

'And now keep your word. Oh, Richard, I am so *glad*!'

'I swear you only agreed to marry me so that you could return to

Yorkshire,' he grinned.

'Oh, I have some liking for you too,' she said demurely.

'Despite brother George's whispering?' He ushered her into a bedchamber, closing the door behind them, his voice dropping into seriousness.

'Let us forget what was whispered,' she pleaded.

'As long as there is trust between us.' He tilted up her chin with his forefinger. 'There has to be complete trust between us so that we can stand together against the world! Hasn't it always been thus?'

'Loyalty binds me,' she said softly, and put her arms around his neck.

Their mouths met and fused and she felt desire bubble up in her.

'Your dress — how does it unfasten?' he asked thickly.

'Hooks at the back, but I can contrive.' She broke into laughter. 'I became quite accustomed to dressing myself when I was at the tavern. Oh,

Richard, I never told them that I was leaving!'

'I sent a man to recompense them for the kindness they showed you,' he said, turning her about and fumbling with the tiny hooks.

The bodice and kirtle rustled to her feet and she stood in her thin shift, her long hair swinging across her face as she ducked her head in sudden, overwhelming shyness.

It seemed to affect Richard too, for he began to talk quickly and jerkily as he moved towards the curtained bed.

'I had this chamber sweetened and aired for our night here. The hangings are of Flemish weave. Shall I douse the candles and stir up the fire for us? It's pleasant to lie in firelight and listen to the wind.'

'It's a very nice bed,' she said politely. The bubbling desire had gone and her heart was beating uncomfortably fast. She climbed awkwardly into the bed, shivering at the coolness of the sheets. For a few minutes she lay rigid, closing her eyes tightly. She could hear Richard moving about as he disrobed and then the weight of him as he hoisted himself to the mattress beside her.

'My Lady Anne?' His voice was a whisper, and his breath fanned her cheek as he raised himself above her.

The candles were doused and smoking, but he had let the fire burn low. The chamber was all swirling shadow and the faceless echoes of the past menaced her. She gave a little cry of terror and clutched at Richard, feeling the warmth of his skin. His mouth pressed down upon hers again and her cry was silenced.

It was not as she had imagined it would be. There was no soaring joy, only discomfort and a searing pain and tears wetting her cheeks, and Richard's breath growing louder and faster.

His suffocating weight was lifted and she closed her eyes again, biting her lip to make one pain drive out the other.

'It was not very good, was it? I meant it to be better, Anne. I meant it to be beautiful, but I was too impatient, too rough. It will be better next time.'

'Yes. Yes, of course.' Her voice was small and cool.

'When we are at Middleham we shall have leisure to be together,' he said. 'So much has happened. We need time, my love.'

'Am I? Am I your love?' Her voice shook a little and the tears flowed faster.

'Of course you are!' He sounded faintly surprised. 'I have just married you!'

'Yes, of course.' She giggled and felt the giggle turn into a sob.

'Lord, but I'm weary.' Richard yawned loudly and ostentatiously. 'Will you wake me later when you're rested? I'd not want to waste our wedding night.'

He was being kind and she was grateful, but she sensed vague disappointment in his tone.

'I am not yet accustomed to being married,' she said apologetically.

'It will be better when we have both rested,' he said, and reached out to clasp her shoulder.

He slept soon afterwards but she lay wakeful until the fire had died into grey ashes. She must have slept then, for she woke to his weight on her again, and this time was slightly better for her nervousness had diminished and he was gentler, less urgent than before.

She kissed him and dug her nails into his back as he reached his own climax, but as she began to rise on a crescendo of pleasure there flashed before her mind's eye the decaying heads bobbing on the spiked poles and, somewhere in the background, Isobel crying as she tossed and turned in the heaving cabin.

Marriage meant pain and death. She had no right to think in that way, but she could not help herself.

'May we ride north soon? Very soon?' she whispered.

'As soon as we have attended Mass,' he said, 'and eaten our breakfast. I'll have a litter made ready.'

'No, I'll ride horseback with you,' she said quickly. 'I want us to ride together, my husband.'

'I will be a faithful one,' he said, and in the grey half-light his face was tense.

There was a scar on his shoulder. She touched it and looked a question.

'I had a small wound at Tewkesbury,' he said.

And my last husband had a small dying there, Anne thought. I never loved him. I never wanted him to touch me at all. I cannot forget him though. I cannot forget that he was only 16 years old.

'Love me again,' she said urgently, and pulled him towards her, closing her mind against the spiked and rotting heads.

10

The Great Hall had been hung with red-berried holly, and shining green ivy, and there was mistletoe over the archway that led to the antechamber where she sat on sunlit afternoons. Today the sun gleamed on white snow and there were only the bare thorny stems of the roses against the wall.

Anne sat by the fire, a rug over her knees. She had been suffering from a chill, but it was greatly improved since the bitter wind had dropped and her cough was less painful. She could hear Richard somewhere beyond the narrow chamber, his voice raised in laughter.

She laid aside her book and listened with pleasure. It was always good to hear Richard laugh. For too much of the time he was engrossed in business, and for most of that year he had been in France. The months there had given him little cause for amusement, she thought wryly. They had set out with the intention of invading France and forcing King Louis to acknowledge the Burgundian alliance and had ended with a treaty being signed between the two countries.

'To which I refused to put my name as witness,' he said to Anne. 'I don't trust the French or their intentions.'

'And you told the King so?'

'Plainly but politely. Louis of France is a fox who will go back on his word if he gets the opportunity.'

'Was Edward angry? Perhaps you ought to have been more diplomatic,' Anne said anxiously.

'Edward knows that from me he will always get an honest opinion,' Richard said, 'and as King he has the right to make what treaties he chooses, and the right to ignore my advice.'

'I am only too glad there was no fighting,' she told him. 'All these months when you were away I dreaded hearing of you being hurt. It was a great relief when you all came home safely.'

'I was bred for war,' he said.

'And now must learn the arts of peace.' She put her hand over his own, smiling at him. 'Are you not content to be at home with me?'

'With you and our son,' he said, kissing her fingers. 'Dear Anne! Four years wed and still as lovely as ever!'

He was the only man who had ever thought her so, Anne knew. He was the only man she had ever truly loved or trusted. It was the greatest pity that their most intimate moments were still unsatisfying. Always she promised herself silently that it would be different, and always at the moment of release something tightened and closed up within her and the fear shuddered through her mind. What made it so dreadful was that Richard never once blamed her or reproached her for her coldness. And though she was quite certain that he was faithful she could not help wondering if he ever craved a warmer, more responsive wife.

At least she had given him a son. Edward, born a year after their hurried marriage, was the joy of his father's existence. Anne had never seen a man so besotted with a small child. He spent hours with the frail, black-haired boy, measuring him every month against the wall, patiently teaching him his letters from the hornbook.

'The next will be a girl,' he had said jubilantly.

Anne had nodded and smiled and prayed silently that she would never have to go through such anguish again. She had not thought it possible that one could suffer so much pain and still be alive. There had been no babies since then, but as she was not yet 21 there was plenty of time, and the physician had assured her that her next confinement would be an easier one. Isobel had proved that such a thing was quite possible, for she and George now had two healthy children and she was expecting a third at any moment. A brother or sister for Edward of

Warwick, and Margaret of Salisbury.

There were too many Edwards in the family, Anne decided with a spurt of amusement. Apart from her own and Isobel's sons there was the King's elder son and the King himself. Four royal Edwards and then there were two Richards now, the King having named his younger boy after his brother of Gloucester.

At least her own boy would live out his days peacefully as Lieutenant of the North. Richard was happier in Yorkshire than in any other place and his firm but fair governorship had established peace in the northern counties. The public occasions he really enjoyed were the ones held in York, when he was among men who knew him and with whom he could talk freely.

The laughter sounded again and she pushed aside the rug and stood up. Yuletide was the loveliest season of the year, she thought happily. The roads were clear despite the snow, and the mummers were due. This year Edward would be old enough to enoy their capering.

'There's a rider coming, Lady Anne. I saw him from the window,' a serving woman announced, bobbing a curtsy as she entered.

'Does the Duke know?' Anne enquired.

'I believe he has gone to meet him, madam,' the woman said. 'He's in the royal livery the rider is.'

'Tell cook to prepare something hot and mull some wine,' Anne said briskly.

'At once, madam.' The woman bobbed another curtsy and went out.

Letters from her mother and sister were rare and eagerly awaited. The Countess was with Isobel at Warwick, and Ankarette had written to say that she had joined them to help at the confinement. Dear Ankarette! She had no children of her own and had never troubled to take a second husband, but she frequently left the comfort of her Layford manor to visit her former charges. In a changing world Ankarette with her red curls and warm hug remained exactly the same.

'Anne? Anne, where are you?'

There was a note in Richards voice that warned the tidings were bad. She had begun to shake even before he came in and, putting his arms about her, told her gently that Isobel and her baby were dead.

'It's not true. Isobel is stronger than I am,' she said blankly. 'She never ailed, save when her first child was born and we were on the sea then and in great trouble! Isobel is strong.'

'Childbirth is dangerous, my love, even for the strong,' Richard said.

'But she was not yet five and twenty. That is too young to die,' she gasped out.

'Many die young.' He sounded old and resigned and she looked at him in fear, crying,

'Not everybody! Not us! We will live to be old, won't we, Richard? We'll not die like Isobel.'

And Ned with his head on a pole,

and the little Woodville babe, Margaret, died less than a year after the procession to celebrate her birth had sailed down the river.

'My brother is beside himself with grief,' Richard said. 'He neither eats nor sleeps, but cries out that witchcraft is responsible.'

'Witchcraft? Oh, Richard, surely not!' Anne gave a sob of fear.

'Of course it is not,' he said. 'But George was always ready to fling wild accusations about. And he did love Isobel.'

'Those two poor little children!' Anne began to cry softly.

'Your mother is caring for them,' Richard told her, 'and you may depend on it that my own mother will do her share of spoiling them.'

'Poor Isobel! She was so pretty.' Anne wiped her eyes and attempted a somewhat watery smile. It did no good to sink into grief. Richard was upset on his brother's account without having to comfort his wife as well.

'Will you go to Warwick?' she asked.

He considered a moment and then shook his head.

'She is already buried and Masses are being sung. I wish I could be with George but he is perhaps better left to wrestle alone with his sorrow. And I have duties here to attend that will keep me occupied until summer.'

She nodded, knowing how seriously he took his responsibilities. There were the estates to administer, the frontier fortresses along the Scottish borders to be victualled and repaired, judicial matters to be settled. He was frequently away for days at a time at Pontefract or Sandal or at Sheriff Hutton where his two bastards were being reared. Anne had never seen the children and the fact of their existence was not spoken of at Middleham.

She had striven since their wedding to create at Middleham a haven of peace where the powerful and often harrassed Duke could be a husband and father, and she suspected that the castle represented for him a refuge where he could be an ordinary man with a wife and son to whom he was devoted.

Isobel's death was a sad start to the year but worse was to follow, ripping apart the fragile veil of contentment that had shielded them from the face of reality.

The first months had passed placidly. Yuletide and Easter and the Feast of Corpus Christi marked the slow decay of winter and the coming of spring, and spring itself yielded to summer. Anne was always glad to see the bright flowers spring upon the surrounding moors and to know the harvest was likely to be a good one. The only word from the Court was that the Queen had borne a son.

'Eight children and they say she is as beautiful as ever!' Anne envied.

'She paints overmuch,' Richard informed her.

Anne thought that she would not grumble about having to use a little paint if she could provide Richard with eight children as easily as the Woodville woman gave babes to the King. The eldest boy had his own miniature Court at Ludlow, but the little Duke of York and the new baby and the four surviving princesses were still with their mother. Anne stifled a sigh and turned to gaze through the window into the garden where four-year-old Ned bestrode a painted horse. He had a real pony of his own which he adored but the animal was too strong for the delicate, elf-like child to manage alone.

Afterwards she was to look back at that day as the calm before the storm, the halycon blue before the darkness.

'Anne, I have to go to London at once!' Richard entered her solar without ceremony, brusquely waving away her maid, who was helping her sort silks for a new kirtle. His face was black with temper and she jumped nervously to her feet, scattering the material. It was so rare for him to lose his poise that she guessed at once something of the utmost seriousness had occurred.

'George is in the Tower,' he said.

'In the — ? Your brother? You mean as a prisoner!'

'Held on suspicion of treason.' He pressed her down into her chair again. 'It is nonsense, of course. Louis of France informed my brother Edward that George seeks to marry Mary of Burgundy and then launch an invasion of England in order to seize the crown. I knew I was right to speak against the treaty! The French seek to set brother against brother, and the Woodvilles are hand in glove with them. It is malicious rumour, gossip and hearsay, and George makes matters worse by flinging accusations in all directions and taking the law into his own hands. He has hanged poor Ankarette on suspicion of having poisoned Isobel.'

'What!' Her voice came out so weakly that it felt like a breath upon the air, but her white face and huge, horror-struck eyes stilled his tirade.

'I ought to have broken it to you

more gently,' he reproached himself, kneeling to chafe her hands. 'I forgot that she had been your nurse.'

'Mine and Isobel's,' she said. 'She is — was one of the kindest people I ever knew. Poisoned, you said? But Isobel died in childbed! Ankarette would never have harmed anybody. It can't possibly be true. There has been some miscarriage of justice!'

'It seems that 80 of George's henchmen went to Ankarette's house and bore her to Warwick where she was charged, tried, sentenced and hanged by nightfall. My brother took the law into his own hands, I fear, but he is not himself! I fear that Isobel's death has preyed upon his mind.'

'Hanged! Dear God!' Anne hid her face and shuddered.

'It is a terrible thing. There must be more behind it,' Richard said, beginning to pace the room.

Anne was silent, remembering. It was Ankarette who had told Richard where Anne was hidden away and, though

George of Clarence had apparently accepted the marriage, Anne wondered how much he had secretly resented the fact that his private plans had been thwarted. The spoilt young man who had wanted to be King had depths to his nature that frightened her.

'You said that he was in the Tower.' She raised her head and spoke calmly and steadily. 'That he plotted to seize the crown?'

'I'll not believe it!' Richard slammed his fist into the palm of his hand. 'I'll not believe it! The Woodvilles are at the bottom of this. Some of George's servants have been arrested on a charge of using magical arts against the King.'

'But it was George who first spoke of witchcraft when Isobel died.'

'Aye, there's something behind all this,' he said moodily. 'Would to God I'd gone down to Warwick sooner! I might have been able to talk to George, to dissuade him from whatever course of action he had in mind.'

Anne doubted if George could ever

be dissuaded from following his own course of action. He had always done exactly as he pleased, turning and twisting and being consistent only in his affection for Isobel.

'I ought to have gone to Warwick after Isobel died,' he repeated. 'George is my brother and when he needed my help I stayed at home, immersed in my own duties, my own occupations.'

'You cannot blame yourself.' Anne rose swiftly and went to him. 'George is a grown man, older than yourself. He must stand on his own feet, my love.'

'With the Woodvilles ranged against him and my brother the King influenced entirely by his queen! My brother of Clarence needs friends now more than he ever needed them before.'

He had on his face the determined expression that brooked no opposition.

'So you will go to London?' She kept her own voice calm and reasonable. 'Will you make inquiry into Ankarette's death as well as George's arrest?'

'The idea that Isobel was poisoned

must have been put into his head by somebody,' Richard said darkly.

'But Ankarette would never have hurt Isobel! She loved us both.'

'George must have been led to believe evil of her,' Richard said. 'He must have been half demented to have taken the law into his own hands. I must go south at once, Anne. I must see George and speak to the King in private without his Woodville councillors standing by.'

'Whatever your brother of Clarence has done the King will forgive him,' Anne soothed.

'Whatever George has done he has been driven to it by the machinations of the Woodvilles,' Richard told her.

Anne was silent. All her life she seemed to have heard people fulminating against the ambition of the Woodvilles, yet it was surely George of Clarence whose ambitions were overweening. She remembered how swiftly he had deserted King Edward in the hope of having her father set him upon the throne and how quickly he had changed side again. She remembered how he had convinced her of Richard's sinister intentions and so persuaded her into hiding.

But it would do no good to remind Richard of any of that. She had learned that her husband had curiously blank spaces in his common sense. No Woodville ever did anything right and whatever George of Clarence did was to be forgiven!

'Will you send me word of what has happened?' she asked.

'As soon as I can. Oh, Anne, I had looked forward to spending the summer with you and Ned.' He put his arms about her and she clung to him, but when she raised her eyes he was staring bleakly beyond and she knew that he had room in his mind only for his brother of Clarence.

Her contentment was fled and it was with a heavy heart that she watched him ride over the drawbridge and down the steep hill to the village. They were so safe here, hidden away in the folds of the moors. The south was a place of treachery and when Richard travelled there she always had the queer, illogical feeling that when he returned he would have changed in some indefinable way.

During the months that followed she received only brief and occasional letters from him. He addressed her as his 'trusty and beloved wife' and signed himself as her 'faithful and loving lord', but for the rest he might have been writing to his secretary.

'Prince Edward of York is to be wed to the Lady Anne Mowbray after Yuletide and there will be a tournament to mark the marriage. I am bidden by His Grace to remain at Court until Candlemas, and so will see you and our dear son at that time.'

No word of regret for not being at Middleham for Yule. No invitation for her to join him at Court. She could understand that he wanted to keep his wife and son unstained by corruptions of the Woodville Court, but a word of regret, a sentence of longing, would have been so welcome.

Anne sighed and read the paragraph again. The King's younger son was only four and his prospective bride was three, but the marriage would bind together the royal line with the powerful clan of the Norfolks. Nobody would ask the children for their opinions, of course.

She folded the letter carefully, wishing he had told her something about the Duke of Clarence, but Richard was discreet even in his private letters. He had informed her briefly that the verdict 'guilty' pronounced upon Ankarette had been quashed and her relatives recompensed, but that wouldn't bring poor Ankarette back. Anne put her hand to her slender neck, feeling a pulse beating in it like a tiny, fluttering bird. Death by rope must be a fearsome thing.

To shake off the nameless fears that pressed her down she moved to the table and rang the engraved silver bell on it. She would have her horse saddled and ride out into the meadows where the only sounds were of birds and breeze and the children who ran from the cottages to stare at her were barefoot and sunburned, with nothing to worry them save the constant threat of famine and disease.

The summer wore on, the harvest an excellent one, the Michaelmas Fair a riot of colour and noise with swinging boats that rode high in the sky, and booths piled with fairings. Anne visited the fair, riding in a wheeled and hooded carriage with Ned bouncing up and down beside her. At each side a dozen gentlemen rode as escort. She recalled how she had jostled among the crowds on the bank to watch the river procession, and thought how surprised the people here would be if she jumped out of her carriage and began to act like an ordinary person.

At her side Ned pointed to some long-tailed monkeys swinging from a painted rail and cried excitedly,

'Mam, oh, Mam, I want one! May I have a monkey?'

'If you wish.' She smiled at him, knowing that he was indulged but unable to deny him. He was so little and so frail that her heart contracted when she looked at him, and she prayed silently that he would grow stronger and taller in the clean, untroubled northern air.

Richard had sent her a gift of a fur hood, and a brief message to inform her that he was at Westminster tending to business. She wondered if the Duke of Clarence would be allowed out of the Tower to join his family for Yule, or if the quarrel was too deep to be mended. Whatever happened she knew that she would never be able to forgive George for what he had done to Ankarette.

It was mid-February before Richard came back to Middleham and she knew as he rode with his knights beneath the covered way that this time he had returned in different case. More than the cold and fatigue of a long journey had sharpened his features and carved grim lines at the corners of his mouth. He dismounted and strode past her into the Great Hall, ignoring the welcome cup in her hands. She passed it hastily to Richard's secretary, John Kendall, and hurried to his side, waving the other servants away.

He had flung off his sable cloak and low-crowned hat, and half-turning as she entered, stirred the logs in the fire with his foot.

'My Lord?' She hesitated, terrified by the expression in his eyes, for he stared at her as if she was an enemy.

'Richard, if you will come to the winter parlour,' she said at last, trying to steady her voice, 'there is wine and bread in there for you.'

He frowned, blinked as if he tried to bring her into focus, and nodded, putting his hand towards her. She took it at once, curling her own warm fingers about his icy ones, moving through the looped arras into the narrow chamber where they sat often on winter evenings.

He let her hand free abruptly and sat down, staring into the fire while she poured wine, the neck of the flask rattling against the rim of the goblet.

'George is dead,' he said at last. 'My brother of Clarence is dead.'

She had know it before he spoke and was afterwards thankful that her first feeling had been one of sadness and not relief. She stood, her hands tightly clasped, while he gulped the rich malmsey as if it had no taste.

'I spoke up for him,' Richard said, not looking at her. 'I reminded the King that we three were brothers, sons of the great Richard of York. I begged him, Anne, and it does not come easily to me to beg. But George was my elder brother, already pardoned for his past foolishness. Edward was swayed. If I had been left uninterrupted — but there are Woodvilles everywhere at Court. They whisper in corners, send sidelong glances from one to another, creep and crawl like rats in the wainscot, gnaw at reputations until they are shredded.'

'What happened to him?' she heard herself whisper.

'He was brought before the Council,' Richard said, 'and there attainted for high treason.'

'But there must have been grounds. They would not condemn on suspicion alone!'

'Oh, he had spoken rashly,' he said, shrugging as if some intolerable weight burdened his shoulders. 'He said that he had heard rumour His Grace was not our father's true-born son! God knows I cannot condone such lies, but I believe George was driven mad by Isobel's death. It must have been that. It was some canker of the mind that made him speak so.'

'Yes. Yes, of course.' She answered him as she would have answered Ned.

'The Council condemned him. Milord Buckingham was bidden pronounce the sentence of death. His hands shook like leaves as he read the Proclamation. Edward sat like a stone, not moving. Not moving! And George cried out that there was more to tell, such news as would set all England by the ears, but the guards muffled him and dragged him out. Two days before, at Dickon's marriage to Norfolk's child, Edward had promised me that he would not act hastily. Two days before!'

He flung his empty goblet down to roll along the rushes, and rose, pacing the floor. Anne, her own legs shaking, sank into his vacated place.

'The Woodvilles conspired,' Richard said. 'They whispered poison into His Grace's ear and into George's too. Brother against brother! The House of York tearing itself to pieces!'

'You did all you could,' she said feebly, but he swung about, his face contorted, and cried harshly,

'Everything I did was useless, everything I said ignored. I don't blame Edward. How could he do other than he did, with George's tongue wagging so slanderously, and the Council declaring that he was grown a danger to the realm, and those damnable Wood-villes urging him? On the very night of his execution I went alone to the King's chamber to make one last plea. Anne, I would have done anything!'

'Did you see His Grace,' she whispered.

'Aye, I saw him!' His tone was savage. 'He was in his bedgown, with his latest fancy at his side. A sly-eyed piece called Jane Shore — I've seen her about the Court. His Grace had been drinking. I could understand that too. I might have reached him then, made him understand that for brother to kill brother was the first and greatest sin. He would have listened to me. But the Shore leman was there, in a gown slit to the waist, rubbing her leg against him, and he told me to go away and return in the morning. The woman said nothing. She smiled at him, and he tumbled her upon the bed, and I left them.'

'How did — what happened?'

'It was a private execution. He chose

his own manner of death, saying that he wished to die of drink.'

'But how?' She stared at him.

'He was thrust head first into a butt of malmsey and held down until he was dead,' Richard said. 'Lord Hastings witnessed it.'

'The children? Richard, could we not take the children?' she asked eagerly.

'They are at Warwick Castle, debarred from the Succession, declared enemies of the realm through their father's treason. A girl of five and a boy of three! Enemies of the realm! There was nothing I could do for them. Later, perhaps, we will see what can be done.'

'Will you stay at home now?' she asked.

'For as long as possible.' He gave a deep sigh and came to her, leaning his head against hers. 'You and I and our son, together in the north. But I cannot forget. I never will forget how the Woodvilles schemed, ensnaring George in his own weakness and sickness of mind. And Jane Shore!' His voice shook with anger and pain. 'I'll not forget Mistress Shore!'

'You must eat now,' she said, and he nodded, but his eyes held the blank, blind stare again and his hand was ice.

11

Great Edward was dead. The news, brought from London by relays of couriers, had shocked the peaceful household at Middleham. Richard kept repeating, as if he were trying to force himself to believe an unpalatable truth.

'Dead of a chill after a fishing trip! I saw him last month and he seemed well. Edward gone! He was scarce 40! Edward gone!'

'You did say that he had put on a great deal of weight,' Anne reminded him.

'Yes. Yes, that's true. He was become somewhat corpulent, but I had not thought him in any danger of ill-health. This is a tragedy for the whole country!'

A tragedy for themselves too, Anne thought. The past five years had been peaceful after the horror of George's execution. They had lived quietly at Middleham, Anne devoting herself to the care of their son, Richard governing the northern counties with a firm but fair hand. There had been a war with Scotland which had ended with the recapture of Berwick Castle, a victory that had greatly pleased the King. But he had been furious when Louis of France had snubbed his eldest daughter by refusing to consider her as a prospective bride for the Dauphin. The treaty with France still held, but relations between the two countries were very strained.

'I cannot believe it,' Richard said again, pacing the floor restlessly. 'Edward always seemed — indestructible. Of all of us he was the shining one, the pole star.'

The sons of the powerful Duke Richard and his wife Cecily were all dead now, save for the youngest and weakest of them. And of the daughters only Elizabeth of Suffolk and Margaret of Burgundy still lived. Anne watched him with sympathy, divining something of his loneliness.

Word of Edward's death had been brought by a servant of the Lord Hastings.

'The King has left all to your protection — goods, heir, realm. Secure the person of our sovereign Lord Edward V and get you to London.' Richard quoted from the letter now and frowned, chewing his lower lip in nervous indecision.

'What are you going to do?' Anne asked.

'His Grace left instructions that I was to be Protector and his wishes must be respected,' Richard said. 'Unhappily the Woodvilles, according to the latest report, have already moved to send an escort to Ludlow to bring the boy to London. They will work to secure the power and the person of our new monarch. My brother's wishes will count for nothing.'

'Then you must do your duty,' Anne said.

Every nerve in her screamed out that he should stay at home and leave the Woodvilles to do as they pleased, but she knew that Richard's burning loyalty pointed him in the direction of London.

'I knew that you and I would think alike,' Richard said, his face brightening. 'I will set out for London at once.'

'You will take a strong escort?' she pleaded. 'Milord Buckingham advised it.'

'I will take no more than 300 gentlemen and I will send word to Buckingham that he is to meet me with 300 more. The Woodville Queen's brother, Rivers, is bringing young Edward from Ludlow, so we can fall in with him en route.'

'Earl Rivers will bring more than 600 men,' Anne warned.

'It makes no matter if he brings 6,000,' Richard said. 'We are not going to invade the south, my love. We are simply going to take our rightful place as Protector of our royal nephew as His

Grace decreed. Oh, the Woodvilles will not like it, but I am legally and morally in the right. The Council will see that and uphold my authority.'

She was silent, hoping that his optimism was justified.

'You must prepare to follow me to London as soon as I send word,' Richard continued. 'I know you dislike the south, Anne, but as wife of the Protector it is your right to be duly acknowledged.'

'Shall I bring Ned?' she asked. Richard shook his head, biting at his lip again. It was a habit that had grown upon him in the few days since he had heard of his brother's death, and she watched it with disquiet.

'Ned may remain at Middleham,' he said. 'It would be a pity to interrupt his education.'

'Yes, of course.' She spoke quickly, aware that Richard would have died rather than admit that the long journey would be too tiring for the delicate ten-year-old boy. The life of his only son was precious to the Duke.

'Everything will be settled when I reach London,' Richard was saying. 'The rule of law will prevail and even the Woodvilles will have to submit to the expressed wishes of a dying King.'

'Yes, of course,' she said again, while inside her a voice she didn't want to hear whispered, 'Fool! The courtiers care nothing for law or for honouring a dead King. They seek power and will employ any means to obtain it.'

'I will send John Kendal back with word when I am ready to have you join me in London,' he promised.

'And dispatch messages along the way?'

'That too.' He kissed her cheek briefly and hurried out.

With a smile Anne thought that she seldom saw her husband when he was not either hurrying somewhere or dwelling with ferocious concentration on the task in hand. It was seldom that he allowed himself leisure to relax, and it looked as if his duties as Protector would take him even farther from home in the future. Gradually and imperceptibly the darkness that had lifted in the five years since George's execution began to close in again.

Word came in the first week of May in a letter written at speed, for it was blotted and untidily penned. Anne who had not expected tidings less than a fortnight after Richard had left read eagerly,

Trusty and well beloved wife,
I greet you from the city of Northampton where I met with Milord Buckingham and Earl Rivers. Earl Rivers greeted me with feigned cordiality, hailing me as Protector and promising that in a day or two we would join the little King at Stony Stratford, but when he was gone to his lodging Buckingham and I talked long into the night. Lord Hastings sent word that in London the Woodville party is arming and that many in the Council fear them. I

resolved therefore to act quickly to secure the person of the King, and, having sent my own guards to detain the Earl, I rode with Milord Buckingham to the King, and found the boy with his half-brother, Sir Richard Grey, and old Chamberlain Vaughan. These I took into custody and ordered their escort to disperse quietly to their homes, which order they obeyed . . .

Anne stopped reading and shook her head in exasperation. It was typical of Richard to give the bare facts with no details or descrption. To have arrested Earl Rivers and then calmly taken the little King and ordered his Woodville guards to disperse must have taken icy courage, but he had not troubled to mention that. She bent her head to the letter again.

. . . His Grace, my nephew, is now at Northampton with me, and I trust to gain his liking by fair counsel. I have heard since beginning this letter that my authority is accepted by the main part of the Council, which news is pleasing. The Queen Dowager is retired into Westminster Sanctuary with the Duke of York and the Princesses, but I have written to promise her fair dealing. Now Lord Hastings prepares to receive us in the capital. We bring His Grace into London in four days' time. I pray you to hold yourself in readiness for your journey south. I commend me to our son and yourself,

Your humble and loving lord,
RICHARD

So the troubles were almost over. Soon the new King would be crowned and anointed, and Richard would be effectual ruler during his nephew's minority. She wished he had sent his love to her in more personal terms, but after 11 years of marriage she was foolish, she supposed, to expect romance from her otherwise affectionate husband.

Despite her fears her spirits rose. Perhaps, after all, her pessimism had been unjustified and it would be pleasant to spend a few months at Court, especially with Richard in the seat of power. She guessed that it would satisfy him very much to be acknowledged as Protector in a Court where he had been despised by the Woodville clique, and for herself a delightful irony in her return as Duchess of Gloucester to the city where she had worked as cook maid.

She would have a new gown, she decided. She had recently been presented with 16 yards of Venetian lace which would make a wonderful dress, the creamy shade of the delicate material suiting her dark hair and eyes. Richard, too, must be regally clad as befitted a Protector. A long gown of purple velvet, she mused, embroidered with gold and white roses would suit him well.

She would have Master Curteys make it for her. Meanwhile there were many matters to attend at Middleham. She prided herself on the good management of her household, on the close personal relationships that existed between herself and her servants. There were the accounts to be brought up to date, some merchants from York to be interviewed, the baptism of a groom's baby, and she must find the leisure to spend as many hours as possible with Ned, who would miss her sorely when she was gone.

Two weeks later an escort of knights arrived to ride south with her. The brief letter from Richard bade her travel slowly and not tire herself, and apologised for not sending John Kendal.

'The truth is that I am so pressed by business that I cannot well spare my good secretary,' his hurried note ran. 'I fear that matters are still unsettled to some extent, but I pray you not to fret.'

That, too, was typical of him, Anne thought. To drop a casual remark and then expect her not to worry! She went off in a rush to check that her linens had been starched and carefully folded in the long travelling cases of wicker straw.

Her journey was uneventful and pleasant. Richard had provided the escort with detailed instructions regarding her comfort on the way south, but though she relished the padded litter in which she rode and the luxurious rooms hired for her use in the towns through which she passed she found it difficult to restrain her impatience. At such a time a husband and wife ought to be together. Her parents had been together in times of prosperity and danger and only when the Earl had left the Countess in France had his luck finally deserted him. She shivered despite the warmth of the sun and willed the horses to move more swiftly.

It was like turning back the pages of a book to enter the city again and look at the narrow streets with high buildings, gable fronts bulging, bells ringing from tall steeples, her escort clearing a path through those who crowded to the doors and spilled out into the road.

The last time she had seen Crosby Place she had worn a servant's dress and been hustled along by George of Clarence. Now she was handed down by a liveried groom and her travelling dress was of sapphire blue velvet. She felt like a richly dressed ghost as she went slowly up the wide steps and down the screened corridor into the galleried hall.

'Lady Anne, God give you greeting!' John Kendal, a sheaf of documents in his hand, came from an inner chamber.

'God give you greeting, John.' She gave him her hand. 'Where is my lord?'

'In the solar, madam,' John began, and stepped back as a tall figure stode into the hall.

For a moment Anne went cold. The young man who had just entered, his yellow hair waving to the shoulders of his crimson tunic, was George of

Clarence grown young and vital again.

'You don't know Milord Buckingham, Lady Anne,' John Kendal began.

'No, No, I do not.' She recovered her poise and gave him her hand. 'I am glad you are here, milord. The Lord Protector has told me of your great friendship.'

'My Lady Anne, the Protector and I stand together in this,' Buckingham said, smiling down at her. 'I have good reason to hate the Woodvilles.'

She remembered having heard that he had been forced into wedlock with the plainest of the Woodville Queen's sisters.

'But you have more friendship for Richard than hatred for others, I hope?' she said.

'He is the one man who can give this realm strong government during the King's minority,' Buckingham said. 'But I'll not detain you, my lady. You are but newly arrived and I know Richard has much to tell you.'

He bowed and strode away, clapping

John Kendal on the shoulder as he went.

'He is so like — .' She hesitated, a frown puckering her brow.

'Like milord Clarence?' John Kendal spoke with the freedom of a trusted servant. 'Both were descended from King Edward III.'

'We were all descended from Edward the Third,' she said wryly. 'I sometimes think it a very great pity that he should have had so many children, for it seems to me that his descendants have been quarrelling ever since.'

'Shall I escort you to the Protector, madam?' the secretary asked.

'I know where the solar is.' Anne smiled and went past him up the stairs. Secretly she felt a little hurt that Richard had not come down to meet her, but she reminded herself that he had warned her of the many matters engrossing his attention.

He was, however, alone when she entered the chamber and, for a moment, as she paused in the doorway, she felt the coldness again as if someone blew very gently at the back of her neck. It was gone directly as he looked up and then, rising, came to her.

'Anne! Did you have a good journey? Is Ned well?'

'Yes and yes. Are you pleased that I am here?'

'Aye, very glad.' He kissed her cheek and her mouth, putting his arm about her shoulders. His brother Edward had been in the habit of flinging his arm about the shoulders of his couriers. She had seen him thus with George when they visited Middleham.

'I just met the Duke of Buckingham,' she said.

'And like him? I want you to like Harry of Buckingham, Anne. He is true friend to me.'

'I had only a few words, being anxious to see you,' she excused. 'Are you well? You look tired.'

'Pressed by affairs of state.'

'And His Grace King Edward? Where is he lodged? I would like to pay my respects to him.'

'His Grace is lodged in the Tower to await the Coronation. I have not made much progress with the lad. He was reared by the Woodvilles and distrusts me, but I try to draw closer to him. He craves the company of his brother of York, so I am trying to persuade the Queen Dowager to let him leave Sanctuary and join His Grace.'

'Have you spoken with the Queen Dowager?'

'Only through the Archbishop. She will surrender him into our custody eventually, but meanwhile she uses the child as a kind of hostage. She is so used to the habit of intrigue that she cannot abandon it.'

'But if the little King is safe and your protectorate assured by the Council — .'

'Not all of the Council are loyal,' he said moodily, dropping his arm from her shoulders and moving away. 'Oh, Harry of Buckingham is a good friend. He was the first to come to me and tell me of the Woodvilles' plotting. They would have overset the last wishes of my royal brother and kept power in their own hands.'

'But the others on the Council?' She tried to remember their names. 'Milord Hastings, Arundel, Northumberland?'

'Hastings is conspiring with the Queen Dowager,' Richard said curtly.

'But it was Lord Hastings who first warned you to secure the person of the King!'

'I believed him loyal.' Richard nodded. 'God knows but he *was* loyal in the beginning! He gave me fair words and I trusted him, but he is a jealous man; he is jealous of the friendship I show to Buckingham. So he conspires with the Woodville woman who sits like a spider in Sanctuary with chests of gold and jewels all about her feet! She was not so heartbroken at my royal brother's death that she forgot to despoil his palace.'

'But Hastings? Have you proof?'

'Letters,' he said heavily. 'Letters

from Hastings delivered to the Queen Dowager by Jane Shore, the trollop who defiled my royal brother's bed and now sleeps with Lord Hastings. The evidence is there. Harry of Buckingham has copies of the letters, names, dates, everything!'

'What will you do?' She tried to speak calmly, but her heart was thudding.

'I have dispatched Sir Richard Ratcliffe to raise my northern troops for the defence of the realm against the Woodvilles. They seek to bring Buckingham down as they brought my brother of Clarence down, but this time they will fail!'

'You must not excite yourself so,' she said, alarmed at his pallor and the clenching of his long fingers. 'If there is conspiracy they can be brought to trial.'

'Juries can be bribed,' he said, and she thought of Ankarette hustled to a rope's end. George of Clarence had brought that about, but Richard had wiped that from his mind, and remembered only the handsome elder brother who had been kind to him when he was little.

'But Milord Buckingham might be — mistaken,' she ventured.

'No. Hastings is a traitor,' he said flatly. 'There are so few of them I can trust. Buckingham, yes, and Ratcliffe and Catesby and Lord Howard. The Mowbrays are loyal.'

'But Anne Mowbray was wed to Dickon of York.'

'The poor little wench has been dead these two years, so that alliance doesn't count.'

The little Duke's bride had died of the measles and there had been a splendid funeral.

'Anyway,' Richard was continuing, 'it was my brother Edward, who arranged that marriage. It had nothing to do with the Woodvilles. What I must do is strike at the heart of the conspiracy. They are not aware that their plotting is suspected. Rivers, Grey and Vaughan are in it too. I sent them north, in custody, but they are in communication with Lord Hastings. Everywhere I turn there is deceit, suspicion, whispering! My duty is to the realm, to my royal brother's wishes, and I am checked at every turn. Buckingham understands how it is with me. He knows.'

'Is there no good news for me, my lord? Is it all plots and counterplots?' Anne faltered.

'One good deed has been accomplished.' He brightened, the tenseness of his jaw muscles relaxing slightly. 'I have brought George's children out of the Tower. Oh, I cannot restore them in the Succession, but I will have them reared at Sheriff Hutton. Poor young Warwick is backward, I fear, but Margaret is a bright little piece. We can arrange a good marriage for her later. The boy must be tenderly treated, for his mind is weak. He's a gentle child, no malice in his nature.'

'You are a good man, Richard,' she said softly.

'Good? I do my duty.' He spoke with sudden harshness. 'All my life I have tried to do my duty, to follow the right course of action. Loyalty binds me! But to whom, Anne? To whom?'

'To the King. To His Grace.'

'My royal brother is dead. Royal Edward is dead.'

'But his son lives!' She caught his arm, frightened by the desperation in his face. 'Your nephew lives and your loyalty now is to him as King.'

'If he is King,' Richard said.

Her hand fell to her side and she stared at him, terror ripping through her.

'Of course he is K-King.' Her childish stammer had returned and she was shaking from head to foot. 'Richard, he's your b-brother's child! His eldest son.'

'But not legitimate,' Richard said.

'I don't understand. Edward married the Woodville woman,' Anne said. She spoke very slowly, carefully enunciating each word.

'There was a private ceremony at Grafton Manor.'

'Recognised by the Church and acknowledged by Parliament.'

'None of whom knew that Edward already had a wife living,' Richard said.

'Oh, no! No, it's not possible! Such a thing couldn't be!'

'Could and was.' He spoke sharply.

'How? Who was the lady?'

'Dame Eleanor Butler, daughter to Sir John Talbot.'

'I never heard of her,' Anne said in bewilderment.

'Neither had many other people,' Richard said with a certain grim humour. 'She was several years older than Edward and already widowed when they met. She would not yield to my brother's flatteries, so he married her privately — three years before he married the Woodville woman. Dame Eleanor and Edward never lived together and she died 15 years ago, but that first marriage was never annulled. The Woodville marriage was invalid from the beginning.'

'Is there proof of the Butler marriage?' Anne asked.

'Not now. My brother evidently destroyed the relevant papers when he married Elizabeth Woodville, and Dame Eleanor said nothing.'

'And can say nothing now because she is dead.'

'Edward granted her a handsome pension and two manor houses.'

'He made various grants to many ladies but that doesn't mean that he married them,' Anne argued. 'You must be mistaken, Richard. If the lady is dead and the evidence destroyed and nobody knows — .'

'George knew,' he interrupted. 'George knew of it and that is why he died. That is why the Woodvilles, to safeguard themselves, worked so upon Edward to have George executed.'

'How do you know this?' She sat down shakily in a high-backed chair and looked up at him.

'A few days ago Bishop Stillington,

he who holds the bishopric of Bath and Wells, came to see me privately,' Richard said. 'He is a quiet man, elderly and timid, not one who seeks personal gain. He told me that in the year my late brother became King he was called upon to officiate at the private marriage ceremony between my brother and Dame Eleanor. He performed the ceremony and was sworn to secrecy, and he remained silent for nearly ten years. Then Dame Eleanor died and the Bishop met my brother, George, and confided the secret to him. There was no proof by then save the Bishop's word, but George threatened to make the tale public, so he was silenced.'

'Your brother appeared before the Council. Why didn't he speak out then?'

'For fear of his children's safety,' Richard said. 'A threat to them kept him silent for a little while, but he could not be trusted to keep silent for ever so he had to die. Stillington was terrified into silence by George's execution and kept silent until now. Anne, he has nothing to gain by inventing such a tale!'

'Have you talked to anybody about this?' she asked.

'To Buckingham and to Francis Lovell and Catesby.'

'And they believe it?'

Richard nodded slowly, his face grave, but there was eagerness in his eyes.

'My brother had a penchant for secret marriages,' he said wryly. 'He wed the Woodville woman in the same hole-and-corner fashion. She had ambitious relatives who brought her to Court so that Edward was obliged to acknowledge her as Queen. They none of them knew about Dame Eleanor.'

'And they will not believe such a tale now,' Anne said. 'It's too fantastic. The word of one man — no proof. Nothing.'

'I believe it,' Richard said, and she saw the stubbornness come into his face. 'It makes sense to me. Good sense.'

'You believe it because you want to believe it,' she dared. 'Because you hate the Woodvilles so much that you would seize at any means to discredit them. Richard, let it lie!'

'And serve a bastard King?' His frown was ominous. 'Is that what you would have me do? Forget what Stillington told me, turn a deaf ear to the knowledge for which my brother of Clarence was done to death? Anne, Anne, how could I do that and be true to myself or to the realm? The little King has no right to wear the crown, for he was not born in legal wedlock, and neither were his brother or his sisters. The Woodville pretensions are set at nought by this.'

'If it is true — and you have no proof!'

'Oh, I believe it to be true,' he said. 'I believe it — deep within me! And I cannot go on without speaking of it. I cannot serve with my whole heart as Protector in the land where I should be ruler.'

'You would make yourself King?' She felt faint and sick.

'No, Anne!' He came to her, kneeling, taking her face between his hands, his voice urgent. 'It is the law that will make me King! The Woodville children are bastard, George's children debarred from Succession, and I am next in blood to my late brother. I cannot ignore that. I cannot! If I am true King according to law, then it is my duty to make the fact known to the Council, to Parliament, and to the people! First I must bring Dickon of York from the Sanctuary. Then I will sound out opinion, ask for guidance from the clergy and the justices.'

'But the Woodvilles are already plotting, you said. They'll not cease because of the Bishop's tale.'

'Hastings must die,' Richard said, and his fingers tightened, driving her rings into her flesh. 'Rivers, Grey and Vaughan too. God knows, it is no joy to me. Earl Rivers is a fine man for all that he's the Woodville woman's brother, and Lord Hasting was Edward's best friend. But their executions are a political necessity.'

All her life she had been hearing those words and now they no longer made any sense. Eyes black pools in the whiteness of her face, she sat and stared at him.

'I promised that I would be a good husband and lord to you, Anne,' he was saying, 'but I never dreamt that I would be able to offer you a crown!'

Rich maid, poor maid, beggar maid, queen. She heard the rhyme jaunting in her head. Rich maid, poor maid, beggar maid, queen.

12

She had never dreamed that it would be so easy. Only four men executed and the Woodvilles still muttering in Sanctuary, the two Princes shooting at the butts on the Tower Green, and the crowds cheering wildly as their newly crowned monarch rode through the streets. King Richard III and Queen Anne. The titles were like titles from some dream of grandeur. She found it difficult to relate them to herself.

The days had passed in a haze of colour and excitement. This was to be the most splendid Coronation ever devised. It would show the entire world that Richard had not seized the crown by stealth or treachery but had been freely acclaimed as lawful King by Parliament and people. There was red and white wine flowing from the conduits and a great throng of paupers given bread, soup and roasted apples at St Paul's.

Anne had been swept along in the pageant of events. They had ridden to the Tower to spend the night quietly in one of the smaller state apartments in the central keep. She had glimpsed on one of the walks above the lawns two slight figures leaning on the battlements to watch them ride past, and glanced at Richard. He had flushed deeply but kept his eyes fixed firmly between his horse's ears. The boy who was now Edward, Lord Bastard and Richard, Lord Bastard, stood in silence to watch their uncle pass beneath.

She had never been in the Tower before and it was a relief to know that they would only spend one night there. She remembered that poor, witless King Henry had been murdered and that George had suffered his bizarre execution here. She wondered if Richard, too, was thinking of those things and guessed that he was, for he said abruptly,

'This is no home for younglings. I will have the two lads transferred to Sheriff Hutton to be with their cousins of Clarence.'

The next morning the great procession formed at the Tower and made its way to the Hall of Westminster. Anne had been borne in a litter of crimson leather hung with curtains of yellow silk, and the noise of cheering, ringing of bells, and saluting of guns from the river made her head spin.

At Westminster she had removed her shoes, and the Countess of Richmond, whom everybody was trying to forget was Henry Tudor's mother, helped her to adjust the train of purple velvet furred with ermine. She was pleased with her dress. Its creamy lace was cut squarely above her small breasts and draped tastefully to show off to the best effect the pointed oversleeves and finely pleated skirt. On her bare head a long veil of lace lay like cobwebs over her dark hair. She had glimpsed Richard, his own purple cloak held by

Milord Buckingham.

The new King wore a short doublet of blue satin, embroidered with gold, and there was an exalted dedicated expression on his face. She wondered if he prayed as hard as she did that they were doing the right thing. Once more as she saw Buckingham her mind did a curious somersault and it was George of Clarence who walked behind the King. There were others there too, remembered from brief glimpses in childhood. The lovely, vague-eyed Elizabeth, Richard's eldest sister, who had been at her uncle's enthronement as Archbishop so many years before; her little son John now grown into a handsome young man; Sir Thomas Stanley whose brother had arrested Queen Margaret and herself but who was now himself wed to the Countess of Richmond.

The chanting of the choirs, the sonorous intoning of Cardinal Bourchier, the swelling chords from the organ, the spiralling incense, all these formed a background against which small incidents stood out clearly. Her purple train was changed for one of cloth of gold which dragged at her shoulders with its weight. The jewelled crown was heavy on her head, and the golden slippers placed on her feet were too tight. She was glad when the long service was over and they were moving slowly along the crimson carpet from the Abbey to the private apartments behind Westminster Hall.

There was a respite here while she changed her slippers and the heavy crown and chain were replaced for a sleeveless overgown of silver tissue and a cone hennin covered with tiny gems so that she seemed to bear upon her head a tower of flashing light. Richard had changed into the long robe that was her gift to him. He touched her hand briefly in passing and for a moment was Richard again, and then they were both surrounded by the glittering courtiers once more and making their way to the Hall of Westminster.

On the dais she and Richard sat in solitary splendour, canopies of state above their heads. The various courses were served on dishes of gold and silver and the food itself looked delicious but she was too tense to eat more than a few mouthfuls.

Halfway through the meal, in a flare of trumpets, the King's Champion, clad in white armour rode into the midst of the hall on a white steed caparisoned in scarlet and white, and cried out his challenge. 'Who is King? Whom greet you as your King?'

For an instant there was silence and she felt the familiar lurch of panic deep in her stomach. Perhaps after all it was a dream and she would wake up in the attic at the tavern with the day's baking to do. Then the assembled company rose crying, 'King Richard,' and the torches flamed into life as the Champion drank red wine from a jewelled cup, poured the rest upon the rushes, and rode out of the company. Rich maid, poor maid, beggar maid, queen.

'Pray God that this reign will be a long and peaceful one,' Richard said when they retired for the night at last.

'It will be,' she said steadily. 'We can make it so!'

'You look weary, Anne,' he said, holding her at arm's length and studying her. 'You are not accustomed to so much excitement.'

'It was a wonderful day. They all acknowledged you as monarch!'

'All who were there,' he said, but his voice was sombre. 'There are others who watch and wait for the opportunity to topple me. But only let me have some time to establish firm and fair government and treasons will wither away. They cry, 'Woe to the land when a child sits upon the throne'. For that reason alone more are inclined to favour my accession. The rule of law always prevails.'

'I *am* weary,' she admitted. 'So much noise, so many crowds! I wish we could go somewhere quiet where we didn't have to smile and bow constantly.'

'Why not go to Warwick and spend a little time quietly with your lady mother?' he suggested. 'I go to Greenwich tomorrow to consult with the Ambassador of Spain. Queen Isabella has offered us a treaty. After that I begin my progress so we could meet at Warwick and continue together to Middleham. You would like to spend Christmas with Ned at home?'

'Oh, yes! There will be so much to tell him!' she cried in delight.

'They say that Louis of France is dying,' he remarked. 'That will afford us an opportunity of consolidating our gains there, and the chance to make treaty with Scotland.'

Anne remembered the ugly, shabbily dressed King who had spoken kindly to her on the day they had married her to Edward of Lancaster. She had been little more than a child, but he had treated her gently and with the respect due to a grown lady. When Louis died a chapter of her life would be finally closed, for Margaret of Anjou had died some years before.

'Our treaty with Burgundy will hold,' Richard was continuing. 'I must make treaty with the Earl of Kildare and see if we can persuade the Irish to stop coining alloyed silver. I want to encourage trade but not at the expense of our own craftsmen. There should be an inquiry into the property laws too. Many honest yeoman are being forced from their land by high rents. Lord! there is so much to do!'

'You cannot begin it tonight,' she said, half laughing. 'Come to bed, Richard.'

'Aye, it's all quiet now.' He stretched and yawned, hunching his shoulder as he prepared to become a private man again.

Warwick Castle was not such a refuge as she had hoped. The Countess, though 12 years had passed since her husband's death, still wore the deepest mourning and spoke often of joining him soon. As she was in the most robust health Anne thought her speedy demise unlikely, but it was wearying to have to listen patiently to her mother's long-winded grumbling. Yet it was hard to be angry. The Countess had built her life around her husband and since Warwick's death she had lived amid the ruins of her existence.

A few days later Richard joined her. The great cavalcade of lords and bishops sent the Countess into a flurry of excited activity but she greeted the King with a mournful,

'You are right welcome, Sire, though I fear in my precarious state of health I cannot entertain you as I wish.'

'I am sure you will contrive, Madam,' Richard said, hiding a smile. 'We were sorry you could not attend the Coronation ceremony.'

'I could not have withstood the journey,' the Countess said sadly, 'but it is kind of you to spare my daughter to me.'

'Was your journey a good one?' Anne asked Richard.

'Excellent.' He put his arm about her

shoulders, beaming at her. 'I have been so pleased by the reception afforded me. At Oxford I listened to two disputations, one on theology and the other on philosophy. It was most erudite. They argued so cogently that I think I could have stayed and listened to them for a week. To spend one's life in halls of learning — but there! I was bred as a prince, not a scholar!'

'Milord Buckingham is not with you?' She glanced past him into the body of nobles thronging into the hall to be greeted by the Countess.

'Harry stayed in London for a week to clear up some business,' Richard told her. 'I met him at Gloucester on his way to his Brecon estates. He has been neglecting his own affairs on my account. I have named him as Constable of England and Great Chamberlain and granted him the Bohun estates.'

'Fifty manors!' the Countess said, joining them.

'I gave the same number to Norfolk

together with the Admiralty of England,' Richard informed her. 'I wish to reward my friends, madam, and win my enemies to me by fair dealing. This reign is to be a just and prosperous one. I am determined on that.'

'It will be so,' the Countess said. 'God grant that I am here to see it.'

From Warwick they moved to Leicester and thence to Nottingham and on to Pontefract. Their son was waiting for them there, and Anne's heart leapt with joy as she held the slim, dark-eyed boy. Ned had grown in the three months they had parted from him at Middleham and his cheeks were red, his eyes bright, his words tumbling over one another.

'Is it true that you are now King, my lord father? My tutors told me so, and the Aldermen of York have given me many presents. White wine and red wine, and white coneys, tame ones. Two lovely white ones but now they are grown to 24.'

'That happens with coneys, my son,'

Richard said, laughing. 'Tell me how you spent the summer, Ned. Are you doing well at your fencing? We have wonderful reports of your prowess at your books, but you must develop your knightly skills. In a few days you will be invested in York as Prince of Wales. That proud title is reserved for the eldest son of the King and brings with it certain responsibilities. Being a King brings more, and those, too, you will bear in God's good time.'

'But not for many years yet,' Anne said quickly. 'You will not be 31 for another month, and I intend to make certain that you live to be 80.'

'Then I shall never get the chance to be King!' Ned exclaimed indignantly.

The ceremonies at York were almost as magnificent as the Coronation itself. Anne had chosen to wear her lace gown again and a circle of diamonds glittered on her head. She had never felt more content than at the moment when she and Richard sat on twin thrones of gilt and watched Ned clad in crimson satin with a wreath of golden leaves on his head kneel before them. He was, she thought, a beautiful boy, as sweet tempered as he was comely. They had been right to bring him up in the north away from the smoke and bustle of the city. Later when he had outgrown the vulnerable years of early adolescence, he could travel to London and there be presented to the people as their future King.

After the long years of quietness it was exhilarating to embark upon a round of feasts and pageants. Anne was amused to receive not only gifts from the citizens of York, but also long ballads extolling her beauty.

'It is odd,' she remarked one morning, 'that until I was crowned not a soul thought me beautiful!'

She glanced up through her lashes but Richard was engrossed in his papers, and only grunted.

'Are you very busy, my lord?' She put down her own book and went over to him.

'Accounts.' He frowned at them for a moment. 'I never knew a monarch had so many expenses to defray. I think we will have to raise John Kendall's salary. Sixpence a day more and an annuity of £80 when he retires from my service?'

'That would be generous of you,' she said, leaning over his shoulder. 'What's this? Master Filpot, bricklayer of Twicknam, £46?'

'His house was burned down and all his goods lost,' Richard said. 'There are so many poor folks in need, Anne. I want to help where I can. I am going to set up a sub-branch of the Council to inquire into the wrongs of the poorer classes. They are too often exploited and ground down. We who hold great power must also protect the weak. Justice can only work if it is based upon morality.'

'You cannot reform the entire realm all at once,' Anne chided.

'I want to be a good King,' he said, brooding over the papers piled high before him on the flat-topped desk. 'I

310

want to leave a prosperous and secure land for Ned to rule. I am determined upon it.'

'But you drive yourself too hard,' she began.

'And always will, so you may cease your nagging.' He reached up to pull at a strand of her long hair.

'Then I shall be glad when we get to Middleham for a private Yuletide,' she said.

'Sire, are you free to receive messengers from London?' John Kendall inquired, hurrying in.

'Yes, yes. I'll see them in the audience hall.' Richard laid down his quill and rose.

'It is near dinner-time. Don't let him stay talking while his meat grows cold,' Anne said.

'Take no notice of her,' Richard said, clapping his secretary on the shoulder. 'She nags from morn till night as if I were six years old.'

They went out together and Anne resumed her reading. It was one of the new printed volumes that Master Caxton was producing, and both she and Richard were deeply interested in the new invention. He was convinced that it would be a great help to the spread of learning.

'Anne! Anne, are you still there?' Richard's voice was so sharp that she jumped nervously and let the book fall.

'What is it?' She was on her feet, but he had returned and there was such misery in his face that she gasped out,

'Ned? Something has happened to Ned?'

'It's Harry of Buckingham,' he said, and gave a curious sob that was almost laughter. 'Harry has raised a rebellion against me. He has conspired with the Woodvilles to place Henry Tudor on the throne.'

'Oh, no.' She stood, shaking her head dumbly.

'He turned against me,' Richard said, and his voice had a strangled sound as if he choked upon the words. 'I thought he was my friend, Anne. I thought he was my friend and he turned against me. He conspired with Stanley and his wife, and with Bishop Morton, and the Woodville Queen. She promised to marry off her girl, Lady Bess to Henry Tudor as soon as he had secured the throne.'

'But what of Edward and Dickon?' Anne asked in bewilderment. 'Why should the Woodville Queen support the Tudor while her own boys still — Richard, are the boys in the Tower still? They *are*, aren't they?'

'As far as I know.'

'As far as you *know*! For God's sake, what does that mean? Richard, where are the children?'

'I left them in the Tower,' he said.

'And where are they now? Are they still there? Are they still in the Tower? You said they were to be reared at Sheriff Hutton. Have you arranged for that yet?'

'Stop questioning me?' Eyes blazing he turned upon her, his face contorted. 'I'll not be questioned by you, Anne! Not by you!'

'What are you going to do? Is it — has the rebellion much support?' she faltered.

'God knows! I have to get back to London at once!' He walked swiftly to the desk and began to rifle through the papers on it. 'There is so much to be done. You had better take Ned to Middleham and wait there for me to send word to you. Lovell will bring out his levies. Norfolk too.'

'You trusted Buckingham, didn't you?' Anne said.

Richard's hands were suddenly stilled, his head bowed over the littered desk. When he spoke his voice was flat and dull.

'I loved him as a brother,' he said. 'He was George come again, bright and uncorrupted by greed or ambition. And he has turned against me, Anne, just as George turned against my royal brother. He has betrayed me and I cannot tell how many will believe — '

'Believe what? What has Milord

Buckingham been saying?'

'There is a rumour spread that the Woodville boys died at my hand,' he said, still leaning over the desk. 'It is said I had them killed so that I could clear my pathway to the throne.'

'But they were declared bastard! You had no need to harm them.'

'No need, and no desire. But the Tudor's claim is so weak that he has every reason to wish them dead and myself suspected.'

'Milord Buckingham has access to the Tower.'

'But the Constable, Brackenbury, is my oldest officer. He would never stoop to the murder of two children.'

'Unless he were convinced it was to help you against some future rebellion,' Anne said with a flash of shrewdness.

'I must ride south at once,' Richard said. 'I must find out for myself if the rumour be true. I must declare Harry a traitor and a rebel. Stanley too. I must — Anne, I'm sorry I shouted at you just now. You didn't merit that.'

'It was my own fault. I nag,' she said, trying to smile.

'If anything should happen to me — .'

'It won't!' she said swiftly, but he silenced her with an upraised hand.

'If anything should happen to me, take Ned to my sister in Burgundy. I charge you with that.'

'Yes. Yes, I will.'

'And take heed to yourself, Anne. I would have you happy.'

'Yes. Yes, of course.'

'And trust me.' He gave her a desperate, pleading look. 'Trust me, Anne.'

'I always did,' she said steadily, and he nodded and went out again without touching her.

13

The rebellion had come to nothing. Norfolk's troops blocked the roads to Kent and Surrey, Stanley prudently withdrew his forces, Lovell struck out for the west, and it rained. The rebels, wet and miserable, trailed back to their homes, and Buckingham had been captured and executed.

Richard had written a starkly factual account of events to her, containing no word of the Woodville boys, no account of his feelings about the beheading of the man he had thought his friend. Instead he told her about the new Parliament that would make men more equal under the law, about the quantity of silver plate he had sold to the Lord Mayor, his proposed treaty with Brittany, a new convoy system for boats going to fish off the shores of Iceland. He said he would be glad to see her in

London at Yuletide, and that faint hint of loneliness sent her south at once. It was a pity that cold winds and lashing rain made it unwise for Ned to travel, but she left him with the promise that at Easter they would return.

She had hoped that when they were alone he would unburden himself to her but they were so seldom private. After Mass Richard occupied himself in Council or with business matters, seldom sitting at dinner or supper longer than an hour. When the morning's business was done he interviewed ambassadors and envoys, inspected companies of archers and pikesmen, was entertained by the wealthy merchants whose great mansions backed on to the river, and at night he was often poring over state papers long after she had drifted into sleep.

Buckingham's name was not mentioned and neither were the Woodville boys, though Richard was engaged in negotiations with the Woodville woman who remained in Sanctuary with her daughters. It must be dull for the girls, Anne thought with sympathy, to be confined thus. She hoped that they would agree to come to Court so that she could show them her goodwill.

'They cannot remain in Sanctuary for ever,' Richard said, on one of the few occasions when he mentioned the matter. 'The girls must be given dowries and respectable husbands and their mother has intimated that she would be willing to retire to some country manor where she could live quietly.'

'You are generous,' Anne said, but he shook his head, moodiness creeping over her face.

'There has been too much enmity,' he said sombrely. 'I would make an end of it.'

He was a good man, she thought, and a good King, but he was not a popular one. His few close friends were bluntly spoken northerners, and he lacked the charm of manner that had brought men flocking to his brother, Edward. Royal Edward had borrowed money from merchants whose wives he had seduced, matched the hard drinking barons goblet for goblet, splashed the nation's gold on pageants and jousts, and been cheered to the echo everywhere he went. Richard excused non-payment of taxes, was notably continent in his private life, and spent long hours on minute examination of government abuses and corruption, but he considered jousting a waste of energy and money, had forced Jane Shore to do public penance as a harlot, and could summon only an embarrassed smile when the crowds cheered him.

Anne wished passionately that more people could see him in his rare moments of leisure, his face lively with pleasure as he listened to a troupe of minstrel boys, or chuckling as he read aloud to Anne from one of Chaucer's tales. Even his humour baffled the courtiers. They were accustomed to a rapier-like, scintillating style of wit, and the King's dry comments, delivered with a straight face, baffled them, for they were not certain if they were supposed to laugh or not. And such moments of humour were rare. There was a darkness about him in these days that followed milord Buckingham's death. His closest friends, Francis Lovell, William Catesby and Richard Ratcliffe could not begin to fill the gap left by the charming and treacherous Duke.

After the teeming winter spring came fresh and fair. The Palace of Westminster required sweetening and the Court moved up to Nottingham, long strings of wagons laden with furniture, tapestries, gold and silver plate, and chests of garments, the household following the litter in which Anne reclined. The long months of winter in the great halls of Westminster had left her low-spirited and irritable, but her mood lifted as the cavalcade left the university city of Cambridge and approached the great castle that overshadowed Nottingham.

'We will go riding together,' Richard assured her, dismounting from his own horse and helping her to alight from her conveyance.

She was so tired after the jolting of the journey that the notion of going anywhere was singularly unattractive, but she forced a smile and allowed him to lead her past the ranks of bowing retainers to the comparative quiet of the antechamber beyond the great hall. There would be a banquet the next day for the magnates of the city and a solemn procession through the town to receive the homage of its citizens, but for the moment they were alone and quiet in each other's company. Anne let her heavy travelling cloak slip to the floor and went over to the fire to warm her hands.

'I have ordered you some jewels from a Genoese merchant to mark your birthday,' Richard said, his eyes affectionate as they rested on her. 'I'm told some of the gems are most cunningly set and there are some very fine cameos.'

'I feel older than 28,' Anne said regretfully. 'Sometimes I feel 40!'

'You look about 16 in that hennin,' Richard informed her.

'It's the latest fashion,' she said, pleased that he had noticed.

'It suits you,' he said, coming to her and tilting up her chin. 'It suits you very well. You look well in anything you wear, though. I have always thought so.'

'I wish you would say it more often,' she said, accepting his kiss with pleasure.

'Fie! if I told you that you looked pretty every time I thought so I'd have no time to rule the realm,' he said, pulling her into his arms and kissing her more thoroughly.

'Do you have any more work to do this evening?' she asked.

'Why?'

'I thought — we might have a private evening,' she said.

'Shameless child!' He gave her the

teasing, loving look that nobody in the Court ever saw.

'Sire? Sire?'

John Kendal stood at the door. Richard still holding Anne, gave his secretary an irritated glance.

'Can't you see that the Queen and I are occupied?' he enquired testily.

'I apologise, sir, but you are both needed. His Grace of York is here.'

'The Archbishop? I thought he was in his diocese,' Richard said.

'I think it would be well for Your Graces to see him,' John Kendal said.

'John, has something happened?' Anne asked sharply.

'Oh, madam!' John Kendal's voice broke and tears glittered on his lashes. 'Madam, 'tis the Prince.'

'Ned? Our Ned?' Anne broke from Richard and caught at the other's hand. 'John, what is it? What is it?'

'The Prince died, Your Grace,' John Kendal said, weeping openly now. 'Four days ago. The physicians thought it only a little chill but it became worse very quickly. Prince Edward died, madam.'

Anne's hand dropped to her side heavy as lead. All her limbs seemed weighed down. Even her eyelids had turned to stone. Dimly, from a very long way off, she heard Richard's voice.

'There is nothing wrong with Ned. There is nothing wrong with my son! I must set the Archbishop right. There has been some terrible mistake. I will see the Archbishop at once and set him right.'

'Madam, sit down.' John Kendal was pushing her into a chair and pouring wine with a shaking hand. The rim of the goblet banged against her teeth and some of the wine spilled down her bodice.

'His head was spiked on a pole,' she said and her eyes burned. 'They spiked his head on a pole, you know.'

'Your Grace, shall I get the physician?' John Kendal asked.

'The physician?' She looked up at him and laughed wildly. 'The physician didn't help my Ned. My son is dead.

My only son is dead of a little cold and my husband had his head spiked on a pole. Oh dear Lord! dear Lord! There is no end, no end, no end!'

She began to laugh more loudly, and in the back of her mind was the echo of Queen Margaret's wild hysteria.

'Madam! Your Grace!' John Kendal, his own grief stilled, was shaking her. All about was bustle and confusion, and the wailing of women. And then there was blackness and a voice crying in her head.

'All gone! All those you loved dead! No help! No help!'

'Your Grace, everything possible was done. Everything!'

That must be the Archbishop, she thought vaguely. She had to blink to bring his face into focus.

'He was only 11, you know.' Her own voice sounded small and polite. 'Only 11 years old. I promised to return to him in the spring, but now I never will. I never will.'

'Madam, the Mayor is here to

express his condolences. Shall I tell him you are unwell?'

Viscount Lovell spoke gently, but she shook her head, pushing him away feebly.

'I will see him. I will see them all.'

'Madam, I wish you would speak with the King,' Francis Lovell said. 'His Grace has scarcely eaten or slept these past two days. He will see nobody.'

'Is it only two days? Only two days since the Archbishop came?'

'Madam, the Archbishop is still here, but the King refuses all religious consolation.'

'I must go to him,' she said vaguely, and then the darkness closed in again. Somewhere in the darkness she was aware of herself, clad in black, receiving various dignitaries calmly and graciously.

'Yes, a terrible shock. His Grace is overwhelmed by grief. I am grateful for your sympathy. Most grateful.'

'Madam you must speak to the King! You must make him understand. He will not accept the fact. He is talking of going to Middleham to spend the summer with his son. You must speak to him.'

The darkness was lifting again and she was so full of grief that it hurt to move. She had cried so much that she was parched of tears and her sleep was broken by attacks of panic that set her heart beating wildly and the sweat running down her. The King had not come to her bed, nor joined her for meals, but she had caught brief glimpses of him as he paced the corridor that led to the chapel.

'Where is His Grace?' she asked.

'In the east turret, Madam,' Sir Richard Ratcliffe said. 'He works on state papers there.'

'Then I'll see him alone.' She put back her shoulders and went out slowly, the train of her long skirt rustling behind her.

The turret room was small and cold, piled with documents and papers, and Richard sat at a table, turning the documents over and over as if he sought something, but when she entered he turned bright, blank eyes to her and said,

'There is so much to be done that one cannot leave it all to the clerks. I have neglected you shamefully these past days, but I will make it up to you when the times are less busy.'

He looked like a ghost, she thought, her face waxen and eyes fixed. One more step and he could easily topple into madness.

'Richard, I have a question to ask.' She took a step nearer, her own eyes unfaltering though her heart was pounding.

'I am greatly occupied,' he began, but she interrupted him.

'I want to know what happened to the Woodville princes. To Edward and Dickon. I want to know if our son's death is judgment against us for the deed you did. I want to know, Richard. I have to know else I think I may lose my mind!'

'Ned is at Middleham,' he said.

Something broke in her then and she flew at him, dragging him to his feet, clawing at his face with her long nails, screaming over and over again.

'Ned is dead! Our son is dead! Our only child is dead! And I have to know what happened to those other children. I have to *know*!'

'Before God, Anne, I cannot tell! I cannot tell!' He seized her wrists, blood running from a deep scratch on his cheek. 'They were not in the Tower. That is all I can tell you.'

'Can or will? Which is it, my lord? Which one? Did Buckingham remain behind in London to carry out your orders? Is this God's punishment on us both? Eye for eye? Sons for sons? Was it all planned from the beginning?'

He hit her so hard that she reeled against the wall. For a moment they stared at each other and then Richard swept all the papers off the table and cried,

'Ned died, Anne! My little son died

and there is nothing left!'

'You have two other children,' Anne said. 'You have a daughter of 15 and a son of 14, at Sheriff Hutton.'

'Katherine and John? They are bastards,' he said.

'Flesh of your flesh. Bone of your bone. You have a love for them that you never speak about to me, and their mother pleasured you once. You must send for them. The girl is old enough to make a good marriage and the lad should have some title save bastard. They are as much your children as Ned ever was, though they were born out of wedlock. They will need you.'

'Need?' He sounded bewildered, the word strange tasting on his tongue.

'George's boy and girl too,' she hurried on. 'The boy is feeble-witted but Margaret is bright. She, too, should be wed.'

'My son is dead! My son is dead and you babble of other children!'

'Living ones,' she said. 'They are what matters. There are too many dead children in our lives, Richard, and too many unanswered questions. Too many!'

There was blood on her face but she didn't know where it had come from, and her hands were splashed with red from the dying sun that crept through the narrow window.

'No more questions,' Richard said and began at last to weep.

A few weeks later the black-clad Court returned to Westminster. They rode in silence, even the horses draped in sable, black plumes on their nodding heads. They had been up to York to attend the Memorial Service for the Prince and from York had gone to Middleham, but it had been unbearably sad to ride up the steep hill and catch no glimpse of the slim, elfin child waiting with his tutors to greet them. Ned's clothes had been given to the poor, his weapons buried with him though he had seldom practised with sword or bow, his pony returned to its stable. Anne, finding his old wooden hobby-horse in a corner of the nursery, had given orders for its burning.

Katherine and John had arrived from Sheriff Hutton, and Anne's first feeling had been one of miserable jealousy. The obvious affection with which they greeted Richard made it clear that he had visited them often and taken a close interest in their welfare. The girl was dark and pretty, the boy sturdy with a tinge of red in his hair. They behaved towards her with the greatest respect, but she could tell they were much more at their ease with Richard.

'The Earl of Huntingdon's son has made an offer for Katherine,' Richard told her, 'and the girl professes herself willing.'

'It would be a good match,' Anne agreed.

'It would bind the Pembrokes more closely,' he said thoughtfully. 'Sooner or later the Tudor will make his bid for the throne and we shall need friends.'

'His claim is so weak,' she frowned.

'Which matters not at all if he can

drum up support,' Richard said moodily. 'I shall do what I can to keep the defences of the realm as strong as possible, and for the rest I rely on my conciliation.'

Anne said nothing. Richard had kept the wavering Lord Stanley at his side and was still on terms of friendship with Northumberland, though the former was the Tudor's stepfather and the latter interested only in his own concerns. No monarch could have been more lenient, but there were moments when she doubted if that was enough.

'I shall name young Lincoln as my heir,' Richard said abruptly.

She remembered again the enthronement of her uncle as Archbishop and how she had wondered if the vague and lovely Elizabeth wished to be at home with her small boy.

'Johnny is my sister's son and next in blood,' Richard said. 'I shall appoint him as Lord of the North.'

What he was really saying was that he had abandoned any hope of her ever bearing another child. Anne smiled, hiding her hurt as she exclaimed,

'Johnny will be an excellent choice!'

'He is the legal heir.' Richard chewed his lip and said abruptly, 'I intend to return to London within the week. Will you come with me?'

'Of course.' She wondered why he needed to ask.

So they came again to the great halls of Westminster where the entire Court would wear black for a further month in memory of the Prince whom few of them had ever seen.

'Grief cannot be indulged in for ever,' Richard said, with the new, sharp note in his voice that held her at a distance.

It was true, she supposed. Other women lost children and learned to laugh again, and Richard still had his bastards. Parliament was due to sit in the autumn and apartments were being prepared for the Woodville girls, who were, at last, emerging from Sanctuary. Their mother had retired quietly into the country, though Anne wondered if she would stay quiet for very long.

She sat with Richard in the Great Hall, the courtiers grouped about them on the dais and watched the daughters of royal Edward file in. This was the first time she had caught more than a glimpse of them and she watched with interest as they warily approached, the tallest of them sinking to her knees at the foot of the steps. She was a lovely creature, Anne thought, but sadly shabby in an out-of-date gown.

'Get up, Bess!' Richard had risen and gone down to meet his niece. 'You and your sisters are most welcome at my Court. Anne, this is my brother's daughter, Bess. I know she is 18, but I have forgotten the ages of the others.'

'May I present my sister, Cecily, who is 15, Anne, who is nearly nine, Catherine, who is five, and Bridget who is four,' Bess said promptly.

There was a spark of humour in her

grey eyes and the corners of her mouth twitched.

'It looks as if we have acquired a nursery,' Richard said, looking somewhat helplessly at Anne.

'Bess and Cecily are old enough to take their places at Court,' Anne said, coming to the rescue, 'but the younger ones would be happier with their cousins up at Sheriff Hutton.'

'Indeed they will, and John, Margaret and young Warwick will enjoy their company,' Richard agreed. 'Will it please you and your sister to stay here with us, Bess?'

'Whatever pleases my royal uncle pleases me,' the girl said gracefully.

'And they must have new garments ready for Yuletide.' He flicked the girl's robe with a critical finger. 'We will have the young gallants writing love ballads again, eh, Bess?'

'It would afford me great pleasure to see to the new wardrobe,' Anne said quickly.

'Then you will be finely dressed

indeed,' Richard said. 'Her Grace the Queen has exquisite taste. Come! we'll go into supper. A private family supper to mark the occasion!'

For the first time in months he sounded as if he had an appetite.

Epilogue

All about her were hung holly boughs and the bunches of white pearled mistletoe. In the gallery the minstrels played with an enthusiasm made even warmer by the malmsey that had been served to them at intervals during the evening. The trestle-tables had all been cleared but servants passed among the groups of chatting nobles with trays of comfits and goblets of hippocras.

Her new gown of black velvet was embroidered thickly with cloth of gold thread, its hanging sleeves lined with emerald. Her hair was bound in a coif of golden net and there was a coronet of emeralds and pearls set on top. Emeralds flashed green fire at her throat and waist and her face was skilfully painted.

Her eyes, despite all her efforts, strayed continually to Richard. He looked, in her opinion at least, exceedingly handsome in tunic and hose of emerald green under a short cloak of black velvet lined with scarlet and furred with ermine, and his low-crowned cap of black velvet was trimmed with a great ruby set in a circle of pearls. He stood with his two nieces, Bess and Cecily, and his expression was eager and interested. Both girls wore gowns of cloth of silver chosen by the Queen, and their yellow hair was combed loosely over their shoulders. They were gentle, good-humoured girls and Richard was being kind to them, having apparently decided to forget their treacherous Woodville blood.

He was only being kind, she repeated to herself, watching as he bowed to Cecily and led Bess out to dance. She danced most elegantly, Anne thought, and coughed gently as she watched them. The cough had steadily become worse during the past few months, sometimes tearing through her thin frame with a ferocity that had in it a malevolence that terrified her. It was as if she were being punished for some fault that she couldn't remember. Richard hated to hear her coughing and she tried to suppress it as much as she could in his presence, but the effort left her weak and shaky.

'May I bring you some wine, Your Grace?'

Viscount Lovell was leaning to speak with her. She shook her head, giving the King's oldest friend a grateful glance.

'His Grace is in high spirits tonight,' she said brightly.

'There has been too much sorrow,' Francis Lovell said.

'It is good to hear laughter at Court again.'

'The Woodville girls are very lovely,' she commented.

'Indeed they are!' He responded with more enthusiasm than she liked, but she forced a smile.

'His Grace and I are anxious to arrange respectable marriages for them,' she said.

'Of course, madam. Several hearts will be cracked when they do wed,' Lovell said.

Her eyes strayed again to the tall, slender girl in the silver gown. She was circling gravely with Richard, their fingertips scarcely touching. They were not looking at each other at all. Anne coughed again, feeling a flutter of panic under her narrow bodice. It was foolish to be uneasy. Perhaps baseless anxiety was a symptom of her illness, but she could not help herself. Uncle and niece! It was ridiculous to imagine — the cough tore through her again, hurting her throat and chest.

'Are you well, madam?' Lovell asked.

'A little weary, that's all. I think I will rest for a while,' she said lightly.

'Shall I summon your women?'

'Let them alone. A short rest will do me great good.'

She cast another swift, unhappy glance at Richard and Bess and went quietly down the steps of the dais into the covered passage behind. The palace was a warren of arched chambers and corridors, rushes thick on the stone floors, tapestries rustling against the walls, pools of light cast by the torches that flared in their iron sconces at the corners. At night she heard the clashing of steel as the guard was changed, and turned in the great, curtained bed wishing Richard was beside her. Since her cough had grown so painful the physicians had advised him to move to another chamber, lest she carry some infection. It was a wise decision, but it made the nights long and lonely.

'Anne, are you not well?' Richard must have followed her from the hall, and she paused to allow him to catch up with her.

'Are you ill — ' he repeated.

'A trifle weary,' she said, forcing brightness into her voice. 'I shall return later.'

'Shall we sit together for a while?' He took her hand in his, smiling at her.

'We cannot both desert our guests,' she said. 'Go back and enjoy yourself.'

343

'Bess is a good dancer,' he said.

'Most graceful.' Looking at him she thought he was not yet in love with his niece but had reached the stage when he felt impelled to bring her name into the conversation.

'But you are not ill?'

'I actually feel better than usual today,' she said, smiling. 'When spring comes I will put on flesh again.'

'Of course you will,' he said heartily. For a moment they looked at each other, each reading the lie in the other's eyes. Then he said, quick and low,

'We have been happy together, haven't we, Annie?'

'Most happy,' she returned.

'And you are not feeling — ?'

'Lord! how men fuss!' She gave him a little push. 'Go and entertain your guests, do!'

He nodded and went off down the corridor. She stifled a cough, feeling the salt taste of blood rise in her throat but, when he glanced back, she waved her hand and smiled.

Aftermath

Queen Anne Neville died on 16 March 1485, during an eclipse of the sun in the 29th year of her age. The King, who wept openly during the funeral, was soon denying that he intended to marry his niece, Elizabeth. On 22 August in that same year King Richard III was killed at Bosworth, fighting against the invading Henry Tudor. With him died Sir Richard Ratcliffe and John Kendal. Viscount Lovell escaped to his own house where he is said to have been inadvertently locked into a cellar and starved to death. Lord Stanley brought out his troops in support of his stepson, and Northumberland stayed at home.

The fate of the two Woodville Princes and their probable murderer remains unknown. The new King, Henry VII, married Elizabeth, Richard's niece, thus uniting the red rose and the white.

George of Clarence's son, the Earl of Warwick, was executed for treason in 1478 and his sister, Margaret of Salisbury, was sent to the block in 1541. The Countess of Warwick died, full of years and honours, at the age of 80.